'Wolfe has also been hired as your personal bodyguard for the duration of the investigation.'

The breath stalled in Ava's lungs and the room spun. 'I don't think I heard you correctly, sir.'

Neither had Wolfe.

Her *personal* bodyguard?

He glanced at Ava's shocked expression and hoped his own didn't mirror it. The King had requested that he organise personal security for her—not that he be responsible for her himself.

'Wolfe is clearly too busy, sir. But I'm sure there's another person out there just as capable.'

She was right about him being too busy, Wolfe thought, but there really was no one else he would trust with her life. Wolfe wasn't sure about anything right now except two things: his need for this woman was stronger than it had ever been, and taking on the role as her personal bodyguard was absolute insanity.

From as far back as she can remember **Michelle Conder** dreamed of being a writer. She penned the first chapter of a romance novel just out of high school, but it took much study, many (varied) jobs, one ultra-understanding husband and three very patient children before she finally sat down to turn that dream into a reality.

Michelle lives in Australia, and when she isn't busy plotting loves to read, ride horses, travel and practise yoga.

Recent titles by the same author:

LIVING THE CHARADE
HIS LAST CHANCE AT REDEMPTION
GIRL BEHIND THE SCANDALOUS REPUTATION

Did you know these are also available as eBooks?
Visit www.millsandboon.co.uk

DUTY
AT WHAT COST?

BY
MICHELLE CONDER

MILLS
BOON

First published in Great Britain 2013
by Mills & Boon, an imprint of Harlequin (UK) Limited.
Harlequin (UK) Limited, Eton House, 18-24 Paradise Road,
Richmond, Surrey TW9 1SR

© Michelle Conder 2013

ISBN: 978 0 263 90035 4

Harlequin (UK) policy is to use papers that are natural, renewable
and recyclable products and made from wood grown in sustainable
forests. The logging and manufacturing process conform to the
legal environmental regulations of the country of origin.

Printed and bound in Spain
by Blackprint CPI, Barcelona

DUTY
AT WHAT COST?

To Paul, with love.

And "a big kiss" to Anne-Emmanuelle
for her wonderful friendship and even more
wonderful French translations. Thank you.

CHAPTER ONE

AVA GLANCED OUT of the car window at the sparkling summer sunshine bouncing off the exquisite French countryside and wished herself a thousand miles away. Maybe a million. That would land her on another planet where no one knew her name. Where no one knew the man her father had expected her to marry was about to marry another woman, and felt sorry for her in the process.

'It's time you stopped messing around in Paris, my girl, and came home to Anders.'

That particularly supportive comment had come only this morning, making her blood boil. His condescending words filled her head, drowning out the singer on the car radio who was warbling about wanting to go home. Home was the last place Ava wanted to go.

Not that her father's anger was entirely unexpected. Of course he was disappointed that the man she had been pledged to marry since she was a child had fallen in love with someone else. The way he'd spoken to her—*'A woman your age doesn't have time to waste!'*—as if turning thirty in a year meant that she was over the hill—made it seem as if it was her fault.

But Ava *wanted* to fall in love! She *wanted* to get married! She just hadn't wanted to marry Gilles—a childhood friend who was more like a brother to her than her own—and he hadn't wanted to marry her. The problem was they had played along with their fathers' archaic pledge for a little too long, sometimes using each other for a fill-in date when the need arose.

Oh, how her father would love to hear *that*… Somehow, after her mother's death fifteen years ago, her relationship with him had disintegrated to the point where they barely spoke, let alone saw each other. Of course if she had been born a boy things would have been different.

Very different.

She would have had different choices. She would have been Crown Prince, for one—and, while she had no wish at all to rule their small European nation, she would at least have had her father's respect. His affection. Something.

Ava gripped the steering wheel of her hatchback more tightly as she turned onto the narrow country lane that ran alongside Château Verne, Gilles's fifteenth-century estate.

For eight years she had lived a happy, relatively low-key existence in Paris; finishing university and building her business, stepping in at royal functions when her brother Frédéric had been absent. Now that Gilles, Marquis de Bassonne, was set to marry a friend of hers, she had a bad feeling that was all about to change.

Ava crinkled her nose at her uncharacteristically gloomy mood. Gilles and Anne had fallen in love at first sight two months ago and were happier than she'd ever seen either one of them before. They completed each other in a way that would inspire songwriters and she wasn't jealous.

Not at all.

Her life was rolling along just fine. Her art gallery, Gallery Nouveau, had just been reviewed in a prestigious art magazine and she was busier than ever. It was true that her love-life was a little on the nonexistent side, but her break-up three years ago with Colyn—the man she had believed she would eventually marry—had left her emotionally drained and a little wary.

At nearly twenty years her senior he had seemed to her to be the epitome of bourgeois intellectualism: a man who didn't care about her heritage and loved her for herself. It had taken a couple of years to figure out that his subtle criticisms of her status and his desire to *'teach'* her all that he knew made him as egotistical and controlling as her father.

And she really wished he hadn't popped into her mind, because now she felt truly terrible.

The only other times she'd felt this miserable had been during gorgeous evenings wandering by herself along the Seine, when she was unable to avoid watching couples so helplessly in love with each other they couldn't walk two paces without stopping to steal another kiss.

She had never felt that. Not once.

She frowned, wondering if she ever would.

After Colyn she had been determined only to date nice men with solid family values. Men who were in touch with their feelings. But they hadn't inspired much more than friendship in her. Thankfully her business kept her too busy to dwell on what she lacked, and if she was getting older…

Pah!

Stamping on even more mood-altering thoughts, she adjusted the volume dial on the radio and wasn't at all prepared when she put her foot on the brake to slow down for a bend in the road and nothing happened. Imagining that she had put her foot on the accelerator instead, she'd moved to correct the oversight when the car hit a patch of gravel and started to slide.

Panicking, she yanked on the steering wheel to keep the car straight, but the car had gathered momentum and in the blink of an eye it fishtailed and rammed into some sort of small tree.

Groaning, Ava clasped her head where it had bounced off the steering wheel.

For a moment she just sat there. Then she realised the

engine was roaring, took her foot from the accelerator and switched the car off. Her ears rang loudly in the sudden silence and then she caught the sound of one of her tyres spinning in midair. Glancing out through the windscreen, she realised her car was wedged on top of a clump of rocks and heather plants in full bloom.

Talk about a lapse in concentration!

She blew out a breath and gingerly moved her limbs one at a time. Thankfully the car had been going too slowly for her to have been seriously hurt. A good thing—except she could picture her father shaking his head at her. He was always telling her to use a driver on official engagements, but of course she didn't listen. Arguing with him had become something of a blood sport. A blood sport he was so much better at than her. It was one of the main reasons she'd snuck off to study Fine Arts at the Sorbonne. If she had stayed in Anders it would have been impossible to keep the promise she had made to her dying mother to try and get along with her father.

His earlier edict replayed again in her head. She couldn't return to Anders. What would she do there? Sit around and play parlour games all day while she waited for him to line up another convenient husband? The thought made her shiver.

Determined to stop thinking about her father, Ava carefully opened the car door and stepped out into the long grass. The spiky heels of her ankle boots immediately sank into the soft earth.

Great. As a gallery owner it was imperative that she always look impeccable and there was no way she could afford to ruin her prized Prada boots. Since she'd decided a long time ago not to take any of her father's money she didn't have any spare cash lying around to replace them. Another decision that had displeased him.

She stood precariously on the balls of her feet and leaned in to retrieve her handbag. Her phone had fallen out and when she picked it up she saw the screen was smashed. Unable to remember Gilles's mobile number, she tossed it back in the car in frustration. She could always call emergency services, but then her little accident would be all over the news in a heartbeat—and the thought of any more attention this week for 'the poor jilted Princess' made her teeth gnash together. Which didn't help her sore head.

No. She'd simply have to walk.

But standing on the grassy verge with her hands on her hips, she realised just how far it was to the main gates. Her beloved boots would be destroyed. Not to mention how hot and sweaty she would be by the time she got there. This was not the graceful and dignified entrance she had planned to make. And if one of those media vans she had seen loitering a few miles back saw her...

Wondering just what to do next, she had a sudden brain-wave. A sudden and slightly crazy brainwave. Fortuitously— if she could describe running her little car into a ditch in such terms—she'd crashed right near a section of the outer wall that she had played on with her brother Frédéric and her cousin Baden and Gilles during family visits to the château in her childhood. Scaling the wall as revolutionary spies had been their secret game, and they'd even scraped out footholds to aid their escape from imaginary enemies.

Ava felt a grin creep across her face for the first time that day. She had to concede it was a tad desperate, but with Gilles's wedding only hours away that was exactly what she was. And, anyway, she had always loved to climb as a kid; surely it would be even easier as an adult?

'There's a woman stuck on the south wall, boss. What do you want us to do with her?'

Wolfe pulled up in the middle of an arched hallway in Château Verne and pressed his phone a little tighter to his ear. '*On* the wall?'

'The very top,' repeated Eric, one of the more junior members of Wolfe's security team.

Wolfe tensed. Perfect. Most likely another interfering journalist, trying to get the scoop on his friend's extravagant wedding to the daughter of a controversial American politician. They hadn't let up all day, circling the château like starving buzzards. But none had been brazen enough to go over the wall yet. Of course he'd been prepared for the possibility—the reason they now had this little intruder in hand.

'Name?'

'Says she's Ava de Veers, Princess of Anders.'

A princess climbing over a forty-foot brick wall? Wolfe didn't think so. 'ID?'

'No ID in her handbag. Says she had a car accident and it must have fallen out.'

Clever.

'Camera?'

'Check.'

Wolfe considered his options. Even from inside the thick walls of the château he could hear the irritating whine of distant media choppers as they hovered just outside the established no-fly zone. With the wedding still three hours away he'd better extend the security perimeters before there were any more breaches.

'Want me to take her back to base, boss?'

'No.' Wolfe shot his hand through his hair. He'd rather turf her back over the wall than give her even more access to the property by taking her to the outer cottage his men were temporarily using. And he would—after he had established her identity and satisfied himself that she wasn't a real threat. 'Leave her where she's perched.' He was about to ring off when he had another thought. 'And, Eric, keep your gun on her until I get there.' That would teach her for entering a private function without an invitation.

'Ah...you mean keep her *on* the wall?'

When Eric hesitated Wolfe knew right then that the woman was attractive.

'Yes, that's exactly what I mean.' For all he knew she could be a political nutcase instead of an overzealous journo. 'And don't engage in any conversation with her until I get there.'

Wolfe trusted his men implicitly, but the last thing he needed was some smoking Mata Hari doing a number on their head.

'Yes, sir.'

Wolfe pocketed his phone. This would mean he wouldn't be able to start the pre-wedding game of polo Gilles had organised. Annoying, but it couldn't be helped. He'd offered to run security for Gilles's wedding because it was what he did, and the job always came first.

Once outside, Wolfe found Gilles and his merry band already waiting for him at the stables, the horses groomed and saddled and raring to go. Wolfe ran his gaze over the roguish white Arabian that Gilles had promised him. He'd missed his daily gym workout this morning and had been looking forward to putting the stallion through his paces.

Hell, he still could. Taking the reins from the handler, he swung easily onto the giant of a horse. The stallion shifted restlessly beneath his weight and Wolfe automatically reached forward to pat his neck, breathing in the strong scent of horse and leather. 'What's his name?'

'Achilles.'

His mouth quirked and Gilles shrugged. 'Apollo was taken and he's a bloody contrary animal. You should enjoy each other.'

Wolfe laughed at his aristocratic friend. Years ago they had forged an unbreakable bond when they had trained together for selection on an elite military task force. They'd been there for each other during the tough times and celebrated during the good. Inevitably Gilles had started sprouting reams of poetry and Greek myths to stay awake when they'd spent long hours waiting for something to happen. By contrast Wolfe, a rugged Australian country boy, had used a more simple method. Sheer grit and stubborn determination. A trait that had served him well when he had swapped special ops for software development and created what was currently the most sophisticated computer spyware on the planet.

Wolfe Inc had been forged around that venture, and when his younger brother had joined him they'd expanded into every aspect of the security business. But where his brother thrived on the corporate life Wolfe preferred the freedom of being able to mix things up a little. He even kept his hand in on some of the more hairy covert ops some governments called consultants in to take care of. He had to get his adrenaline high from something other than his beloved Honda CBR.

'Always the dreamer, *Monsieur le Marquis*,' he drawled.

'Just a man who knows how to have balance in his life, Ice,' Gilles countered good-naturedly, calling Wolfe by his old military nickname. He swung onto the back of a regal-looking bay. 'You should try it some time, my friend.'

'I've got plenty of balance in my life,' Wolfe grunted, thinking about the Viennese blonde he'd been glad to see the back of a month ago. 'No need to worry your pretty head on that score.'

Achilles snorted and tossed his nose in challenge as Wolfe took up the reins.

'I won't be joining you just yet. I need to check on an issue that's come up.' He kept his tone deliberately bland so as not to alarm his friend, who should be concentrating on why he was signing his life away to a woman in matrimony rather than why a woman was currently sitting on one of his outer walls. 'Achilles and I will join you in a few.'

The horse pulled against the bit and Wolfe smiled. There was nothing quite like using all his skills to master a difficult animal, and he wondered if Gilles would consider selling him. He already liked the unmanageable beast.

* * *

Okay, so maybe it wasn't that much easier to scale a high brick wall as an adult, Ava conceded. In fact it had been downright scary and had shown her how unfit she was. Her arm muscles were aching in protest. It hadn't helped when she'd discovered the ancient chestnut tree she had been relying on to help her down the other side had been removed, and then two trained security guards wielding machine guns had happened upon her.

She hadn't considered that Gilles would have hired extra security for the wedding, but in hindsight she should have done. Naturally the men hadn't believed her about the car accident, and now all she needed was for one of those media helicopters she could hear to zero in on her and her joyous day would just about be complete.

It was all Gilles's fault, she grouched to herself, eyeing the uneven terrain at her feet where the magnificent tree had once stood. And surely they'd raised the height of the wall since the last time she'd climbed it as a tearaway twelve-year-old.

Shifting uncomfortably, she eyed the two killers camouflaged in street clothes below, glad she was conversant in English. She knew no self-respecting Frenchman would ever be seen mixing flannel with corduroy. 'If you would just check a couple of hundred metres up the road you'll find my car and realise that I am telling you the truth,' she repeated, struggling to hold back the temper her father had often complained was as easy to strike up as a match. Which actually wasn't true. It took special powers to induce her to lose the plot.

'Sorry, ma'am. Boss's orders.' That from the one who looked slightly more sympathetic than the other—although that was like saying snow was colder than ice.

'Fine. But I have a headache and I'd like to get down.'

'Sorry, ma'am—'

'Boss's orders,' Ava finished asininely, wondering what

the two men would do if she decided to jump. Not an entirely practical option since she would likely break her ankle.

It had clearly been an oversight on their part as children only to whittle footholds on *one* side of the wall. A mistake no self-respecting spy in their right mind would have made!

Ava briefly closed her eyes and gently tested the injury on her forehead. It felt so large she was sure the House of Fabergé would weep to get their hands on it.

A wave of irritation threatened to topple her off the wall and impale her on one of those raised guns, and as much as she told herself it was irrational to be irritated with these men, since this whole situation was her own fault, she couldn't dispel her growing agitation. In truth, she felt like a fool sitting atop Gilles's wall like a silly bird.

'And where is this boss of yours?' she queried, injecting her voice with a calm she was far from feeling.

'Coming soon, ma'am.'

So was Christmas. In four months' time.

A low rumble of thunder brought Ava's head around as she tried to locate the sound. Her view was hampered by soaring parkland trees and wild shrubbery, and the only thing visible in the distance were the rounded red brick towers of the château and a picture-perfect blue sky beyond.

Then a flash of white amongst the trees caught her attention, and she couldn't look away as a purebred stallion galloped into view. Ava's eyes drank in the beautiful creature—and then she felt slightly dizzy as her eyes took in its handsome rider.

Windswept sandy hair was brushed back from a proud face with a strong nose and square jaw, wide shoulders and a lean torso rippled beneath a fitted black polo shirt, and long, muscular legs were outlined to perfection in white jodhpurs and knee-high black riding boots.

She sensed he was absolutely furious, even though he hadn't moved a well-honed muscle. His narrowed eyes were boring into hers with the intense focus of a natural hunter. Even when the horse stamped impatiently beneath him, its nostrils flaring and its tail flicking with irritation, the man remained preternaturally still.

Ava's heart pounded and she found her fingers gripping the stone wall for support. Heat was turning her limbs soft. Of course it was the sun making her hot, not the ruthless-looking warrior staring at her with an arrogance that bordered on insolence.

'Are you the reason I'm still on this wall?' The confrontational words were out of her mouth before she'd known they were in her head and she could have kicked herself. She had meant to be pleasant, to make sure this ordeal was over as quickly as possible. She knew instantly from the firm jut of his jaw that she had well and truly put paid to that.

Wolfe didn't move a muscle as his eyes swept over the fey gypsy on the wall. He'd been wrong. She wasn't attractive. She was *astonishingly* attractive, and his soldier's eyes noted everything. High cheekbones, honey-gold skin, eyes as dark as night and thick sable hair pulled into a ponytail, wisps from which floated around a lush, sulky mouth that looked as if it was waiting to be kissed.

By him.

Impatiently discarding the unexpected thought, he let his eyes drift lower over a white cotton shirt the gentle breeze was using to outline her rounded breasts, and fitted jeans that hugged long slender legs. And bare, stocking-clad feet!

Achilles swatted the air with his tail, as if he too was disturbed by the vision, and then Wolfe registered her haughty, royally pissed-off question and recovered himself. She was an intruder, and she was ruining a rousing game of polo, and if she was upset she could stand in line.

'No.' He shot her a cursory look. '*You* are the reason you're still on that wall.'

Ignoring her hissed exhalation he swung out of the saddle and approached his men. He could feel her eyes following him and wondered at their exact colour, immediately irritated at the irrelevant thought.

He waited for Eric to fill him in on how they had come across her, and then indicated for him to pass over the leather handbag he held in his hand.

'Is the gun absolutely necessary?'

Her slightly bored question floated down from the wall.

'Only if I have to shoot you with it.' He didn't bother looking at her when he spoke. 'And keep your hands where I can see them.'

'I'm not a criminal!'

He ignored her little outburst and inspected her handbag. 'Find anything interesting in here?'

'No, boss. Usual women things. Lipstick, tissues, hair clips. No ID, as I said.'

He heard her exasperated sigh. 'I already told your watchdogs I had a car accident and my purse must have fallen out of my bag.'

'Convenient.'

'For whom? You?'

Wolfe gave her a stare he knew from experience made grown men think twice. 'You have an awfully smart mouth for someone in your predicament.' And he wished she would close it. The husky quality of her lightly accented voice was having an adverse effect on his body.

'I am Princess Ava de Veers of Anders and I demand you let me down from here immediately.'

Wolfe ran his eyes over her again, just for the sheer pleasure of it and because he knew it would put her on the back foot. 'What are you doing on a wall, Princess? Learning to fly?'

'I am a guest at this wedding and you are likely to lose

your job if you insist on leaving me up here. I'm probably sunburned by now.'

'By this watered-down version of the sun?' And on that golden skin? 'Unlikely. And honoured guests usually approach by the main gates. What outlet do you work for?'

Her brow crinkled. 'I don't—'

'Newspaper? Magazine? TV station? Nice camera, by the way. Mind if I take a look?'

'Yes, I do.'

He dumped her handbag on the grass and started checking through her photos.

'I said *yes*, I do mind.'

'Whether I look or not isn't contingent on whether you mind.'

'Why bother asking, then?'

He nearly smiled at the exasperation in her voice. 'Manners.'

She made a cute noise that said he wouldn't know what manners were if they conked him on the head.

Frowning at the photos on her camera, he glanced up at her. 'Nice celebrity shots on here. I repeat—what rag do you work for?'

She rolled her eyes. 'I am not a member of the paparazzi, if that's what you're suggesting.'

'No?'

'No. I own an art gallery. Those were taken at a recent opening night. Not that it is any of your business.'

Wolfe rubbed his jaw and pretended to consider that. 'Really? Given your current predicament, I'd say it's very much my business.'

She looked as if she was holding on to her temper by a thread. 'I do understand how this looks. And I even appreciate how efficient your men were at spotting me—'

'I'm so happy to hear that.'

'But—' she carried on as if he hadn't interrupted '—I am

who I say I am. My car is a couple of hundred metres that way, and your men would already know this if they had bothered to go and find it instead of holding their weapons on me as if I was a terrorist.'

Wolfe handed the camera to Eric. 'Oh, I'm sorry.' He didn't bother to hide the contempt he felt for her type. Haughty princesses—real or imagined—who thought their needs took preference over everybody else's. 'Did I forget to tell you? My men take orders from *me*, not you.'

Her pout turned even sexier. 'Convenient.'

He wasn't in the frame of mind to appreciate her wisecrack and nearly reconsidered his need to verify her identity before tossing her back over the wall.

'Eric. Dane. Take the Jeep and find her car. If it exists.'

She sniffed at his instructions and shifted her bottom on the wall. She must be completely uncomfortable by now. Serve her right.

'I told you to keep your hands where I could see them.'

She rolled her eyes. 'Do you think it might be at all possible that I could wait on the ground for your men to return? I promise not to overpower you while they are gone.'

The air seemed to buzz with the antagonistic heat she imbued him with, and her accent lent her sardonic words a sexy edge. She was a wicked combination of beauty and spirit, and not even the way she spoke down to him was enough to keep his libido at bay. A truly annoying realisation.

'I think I can handle you.'

Her eyes dropped to his mouth and Wolfe felt a kick of lust all the way to his toes. He waited, breathless, for the heat in his groin to dissipate, but if anything it got worse. Then her eyes blazed into his and the chemistry he'd been trying to ignore sparked like a live wire between them.

The way her eyes widened he thought perhaps she had read his thoughts, but that was impossible. Fourteen years in the business and Wolfe knew how to hide what he was feeling—hell, he'd learned how to do that by the time he could walk.

Perhaps she'd just felt the same burn he had. And had liked it just as little, if her wary gaze was anything to go by. Which gave him a moment's pause. If she was a journalist—or, worse, some sort of political stalker—she'd have already used that connection to manipulate him, not shy away from it as if she'd just been singed.

His eyes took in wrists that looked impossibly slender within the cuffs of her masculine-style shirt, then moved down along fine-boned hands and nails buffed to perfection. She didn't do hard labour. That much was obvious.

He knew instinctively she was who she said she was. It was in her regal bearing, the swanlike arch of her neck, in her sense of entitlement and the way she looked at him as if he was staff. His mother had often looked at his father like that and Wolfe had always felt sorry for the poor bastard.

She shifted again, her eyes on the ground. 'Do you have any suggestions on how I might get down from here?' And with a degree of dignity, her tone seemed to imply.

'Perhaps you'd like me to unfold my trusty ladder from my back pocket?' Wolfe mocked. 'Oh, dear. Left it at home.' He opened his hands, palms facing upwards. 'Guess you'll just have to jump into my arms, Princess. What a treat.'

His horse snickered and her eyes used the excuse to glance at the stallion before returning to his. 'Channelling your inner Zorro?' she asked sweetly.

His lips twitched. 'Only because I left my Batman tool belt at home.'

'With Robin?'

Despite his less than stellar mood he chuckled. 'Cute. Toss down the boots first.' The last thing he wanted was to be stabbed by one of those dangerous-looking heels, and by the gleam in her eyes that was exactly what she was considering.

'I have a better idea. Why don't I just go back down the way I came up?'

'No.'

Her lips tightened. 'It makes perfect sense. I can—'

'Try it and I *will* shoot you.'

'You don't have a gun.'

'I have a gun.'

She paused, her stillness telling him she was weighing up whether he was telling the truth or not. Her eyes slid down his torso and over his legs and he felt a rush of unexpected excitement, as if she'd actually touched him.

'You are being overly obnoxious about this,' she fumed.

'Not yet, I'm not.' Wolfe barely managed to suppress his rising aggravation at this physical response to a woman he already didn't like. 'But I'm getting close.'

'If you drop me I'll sue you.'

'If you don't hurry up and get down from that wall I'll sue *you*.'

Her dark brows arched imperiously. 'For what?'

'Trying my patience. Now, pass down the boots. Nice and easy,' he warned softly.

With an audible sigh she dropped her boots one after the other into his outstretched hands. The kid leather was warm from her touch.

'Now you.' His voice had grown rough—a clear indication that some part of him was looking forward to holding her in his arms. And what was wrong with that? He might not be interested in starting up another affair straight after his last one had ended so tastelessly, but he *was* male and this woman *was* beautiful.

'I'd rather wait for a ladder.'

So would he.

'Then you'd better settle in. I run security, not rescue.'

Again she glanced dubiously at the ground. 'It didn't seem

like such a big drop when I was younger. And what happened to the chestnut tree that used to grow here?'

'Now you're mistaking me for a gardener, Princess. What next?'

Her eyes narrowed. 'Certainly not for a nice man. Rest assured of that. And my correct title is Your Royal Highness.'

He knew the correct title. He might not be royal himself, but he'd met enough in his lifetime to know how to address one. 'Thanks for the tip. But I don't have all day. So let's go.' Time to stop thinking about the tempting swell of her breasts and her hot mouth.

'*You* don't have all day? Thanks to you, I'm impossibly late now,' she complained.

He beckoned her with his fingers. 'My heart bleeds.'

'You're really very rude.'

'Want me to leave you up there?' he prompted, fresh out of patience.

'Excuse me for being a little uneasy.'

Wolfe sighed and held his hands up again. 'I've never dropped a princess before.'

'You've probably never had the opportunity before now.'

He shook his head. 'You sure do know how to make yourself vulnerable, Princess.'

She muttered something in French, making him want to smile. She was all fire and...*attitude*!

Balancing on her hands, she carefully swung her leg over the wall, so that she was perched on it like a little chipmunk, her fingers turning white as she gripped the edge. Still she hesitated, lifting first one thigh and then the other to make sure the fabric of her jeans didn't catch.

'Want me to count to three?' he drawled.

She threw him a dark look, her eyes fixed firmly on his, and then they snapped closed and she launched herself off the wall.

Wolfe felt her svelte torso slide through his hands as he

caught her, his arms winding around her before she hit the ground. Her rib cage heaved as she dragged in an unsteady breath, the movement flattening her soft breasts against his hard chest.

Her arms clung tight around his neck, holding his face against the warm pulse at the base of her neck. His senses instantly filled with her heat and sweet perfume. He usually found perfume cloying. Hers wasn't, and was probably the reason he held her longer than he needed to. Held her moulded against him as if he'd been doing it his whole life. Held her long enough to wonder how it would feel to fit himself deep inside her.

Tight. Hot. Wet.

Wolfe's head reared back as his senses took over and he found himself staring into exquisite, wide-spaced navy blue eyes that made him feel as if he'd been hit by a land-to-air missile.

'You can put me down now,' she said a little breathlessly.

He could slide his hands down to her butt and wrap her legs around his waist, as well.

As if he'd spoken out loud the air between them thickened, and he felt every hot inch of her go impossibly still against him.

Almost embarrassed by a stupefyingly strong urge to crush her mouth beneath his, which had held him spellbound for—God—he hoped only seconds, he none-too-gently set her on her feet and stepped back from her.

It was only then that he noticed the slight swelling above her right temple.

'You should get that looked at,' he instructed roughly.

Her eyes licked over his face before meeting his, her breathing as uneven as his heart rate. 'I'm fine.'

'Put your shoes on. It's time to go.' He busied himself with collecting Achilles while his mind came back on line. By rights he should search her, to make sure she was clean, but, *hell*, he wasn't touching her again. Bad enough he'd have to put her on the back of the horse since Eric and Dane had yet to return.

He frowned, wondering what was taking them so long.

'I'd rather walk.' Her eyes flitted from the stamping stallion and back to him.

Realising he was functioning below par, and that had he been on a real military expedition he might well be dead now, Wolfe re-engaged his instincts and gave her a hard stare. 'You can try my patience, Princess, but I wouldn't recommend it.'

She blinked, as if she hadn't expected his curt tone. 'Unlike your men, I don't take orders from you.'

Wolfe widened his stance in a purely dominant move he knew she hadn't missed. 'We have yet to establish your real identity, so you either get on that horse or I'll use one of these reins to bind your hands and drag you behind.'

'I'd like to see you try,' she invited him coolly.

He couldn't believe this posh piece of work was calling his bluff. 'Would you, now?'

She balled her hands on her hips and drew his sight to her slender curves. Not a clever move in his currently cantankerous state of combined anger and arousal. Of course he wouldn't drag her, but he'd subdue her and throw her over his saddle.

He saw the moment she realised his threat wasn't entirely idle.

'Only men with very small appendages play the tough guy.'

'And only women who are incredibly stupid challenge a man they've never met to prove his masculinity. Fortunately for you, I don't feel the least threatened to prove myself by shrewish females.'

'What can I say?' She cocked her hip towards him insolently. 'You bring out the best in me.'

Wolfe breathed deep at her intentionally provocative manner. 'I'm sure that's very far from your best, Princess,' he drawled.

Her brows slowly rose and Wolfe realised he'd inadvertently revealed how attractive he found her. No doubt it was something she was used to and, like all women in his experience, would take absolute advantage of it given half the chance.

Something he didn't plan to do.

Aggravated by his one-track mind, he was about to end her rebellious stance by physically dumping her onto the horse when his phone rang.

'We found the car, boss. She's legit. Her purse must have been thrown from her bag because it was lodged under the front seat.'

Wolfe grunted a reply and told his men to meet him at the cottage.

He looked up in time to catch her superior expression and knew that she'd overheard his conversation. 'Seems you are who you say you are. Next time use the gate.' He brought Achilles alongside her and grabbed the stirrup. 'Give me your leg.'

'You're not even going to apologise?'

Her tone spoke of generations of superiority that made any apology Wolfe might have given die on his lips.

'Your leg?' he repeated, his eyes cool and guarded against the fire pouring out of hers.

Moving forward, she tossed her ponytail over her shoulder, caught her heel on a rock and pitched straight into his arms.

Already highly sensitised to her touch, and not sure if the move had been deliberate, to throw him off balance, Wolfe immediately set her away from him. 'And don't try using that sexy little body to garner any favours, Princess.'

'Trust me when I say that touching you is the last thing I would want to do.'

She presented him with her stiff back, gathered the reins

up in one hand and stamped her foot into his hand. Wolfe didn't know whether to be amused by her or angered, and perhaps if he hadn't been about to head off after Gilles's wedding to oversee an important software installation he might have hung around to test her lofty challenge. But he was, and he wasn't stupid enough to get involved with another highly strung female.

'Shift back,' he grated. No way was she riding in front, where she would be cradled between his hard thighs.

'You know, all that masculine muttering is entirely uncalled for. You are unquestionably the most irritating individual I have ever had the misfortune to come across.'

Wolfe was just about to tell her the feeling was entirely mutual when she twisted the reins out of his slack hold and dug her heels into Achilles's side. The horse responded like the thoroughbred it was and sprang into an instant gallop.

Wolfe couldn't believe it!

Not only had the little spitfire turned him on just by breathing, she had completely got the better of him. Neither of which had happened to him in… It had *never* happened before!

'Dammit!'

Cursing under his breath, Wolfe whistled sharply. If Gilles had trained his animals correctly the horse should come to a complete stop.

CHAPTER TWO

ONE MINUTE AVA was flying across the uneven ground with breathless speed and the next she wasn't moving at all. The horse did little more than twitch its majestic tail as she tried to urge him forward. By the time she worked out what had happened the overbearing *inbecile* was almost upon her.

'Come on, horse. Do *not* listen to him. He is nobody.'

'You look like butter wouldn't melt in your mouth, but you're a bossy little thing aren't you, Princess?'

'You are so arrogant.'

He settled his hands on his hips. 'That's rich, coming from you.'

'I am not arrogant,' she said in a voice that would have made her father proud. 'I am confident. There is a difference.'

He had the gall to laugh. 'And the difference would fit inside a flea's arse.'

Ava used her sweetest voice to call him a foul name in French, knowing he probably wouldn't understand her.

He shook his head and tsked. 'Temper, temper.' His gaze lifted to her hair. 'If I didn't know better I'd say there was a red streak running through that glossy mane of yours.'

A chauvinist. How original. 'I suppose you think I should be flattered you didn't say blond?'

'No, I would never confuse you with a blonde,' he said with mock seriousness. 'I like blondes.'

'Then I *do* consider myself flattered!'

She thought about flicking the reins to try and ride off again, but he read her mind and his jaw clenched. 'I don't make the same mistakes twice. Shift back.'

Ava noticed how big the hand was that gripped the reins and instantly recalled how they had felt on her body as he'd caught her. Once again her pelvis clenched, sending delicious ripples of sensation through her whole body. Surprised, and a little breathless, she berated herself for the physical reaction. He was Neanderthal man two million-odd years later, his blood supply no doubt taken up by all the muscles in his body instead of his head, where he needed it most.

He moved a small handgun out from under the back of his shirt and tucked it inside his boot, and she felt another traitorous thrill shoot straight to her core. Peevishly she hoped the gun went off and shot him in the foot.

'I'm sure many women get turned on by your barbaric tactics, but I can assure you I am not one of them.'

'Good to know.' He stroked the horse's neck in long, smooth sweeps. 'Since I'm not trying to turn you on.'

His eyes glittered up at her and made her heart pump just that little bit faster. Lord, she hoped he didn't know she was lying, because she *shouldn't* find this uncultured beast of a man so attractive.

Grabbing the pommel, he fitted his foot into the stirrup. 'Now, you can ride up in front between my legs if you want to, Princess. Who knows? It might be fun.'

Ava quickly scooted back and ground her teeth together when he gave a low, sexy laugh. His voice was rich and totally indolent, as if he was always thinking of ways to pleasure a woman.

He swung easily onto the great horse, his large frame filling the saddle. The horse shifted as it readjusted to take their weight. 'You might want to hang on.' He shot over his shoulder, drawing up the reins.

'I am.'

He glanced to where her hands gripped the saddle blanket before raising his eyes back to hers. Ava drew in a sharp breath at the impact.

'I meant to me.'

Ava had no intention of holding on to him. 'Dream on.'

He gave a half smile, as if he might do exactly that, clenched his powerful thighs, and the horse sprang forwards as if it had nothing more than a child on its back.

Instinctively Ava clutched at his shirt and found herself plastered up against the back of him. He was hard! And hot! Unable to help herself, she widened her fingers over his abdominal muscles as if she needed to do so to prevent herself from falling off. Colyn had always bemoaned the fact that she wasn't tactile enough for him, but right now she could barely resist the urge to explore this stranger's muscular physique. She thought she heard him blow out a hard breath and, slightly embarrassed at her temerity, quickly moved her fingers to his narrow hips. The roll of muscle there told her that he worked out. A lot.

Fortunately it took no time for the spirited stallion to make it to the main buildings. Unfortunately it was still long enough for the friction from the saddle and his body to make the space between her legs feel soft and moist.

Mon Dieu.

Yes, it had been a long time since she had been intimate with a man, but this one was *so* not her type…

Focusing on her surroundings, instead of the man she could feel with every cell of her body, she realised they weren't at the stables but at one of the side entrances to the main building.

About to ask what they were doing there, she stopped when he twisted around in the saddle, grabbed her under her arm and effortlessly lifted her off the horse. Ava felt the slide of his thigh all the way down her body and closed her eyes briefly to block out the rush of heat coursing through her. When her feet finally touched the ground she locked her knees to take her weight and had to force herself to push away from his heat.

'Any time you want to learn how to fly again, Princess, you just call me, okay?'

Ava curled her lip, but before she could come up with a pithy retort he had dug his heels into the stallion and was gone.

Thank God. It would take two top-of-the-line masseurs to work the tension out of her back after that!

'Ma'am? Are you lost?'

A footman materialised at her side, and it was only then that Ava registered that her 'captor' had set her down in a private part of the castle, far from the prying eyes of arriving guests. It was probably more because he was used to using the servants' entrance than out of any actual consideration for her, but even as she had the ungrateful thought she had a feeling she was wrong.

Wolfe stood on the lime-green lawn at the side of the white marquee set up as a servers' area under the shade of a weeping willow. He wasn't on duty, but his eyes scanned the throng of wedding guests holding sparkling glasses of wine and champagne and recapping the beautiful service they had just witnessed.

The men mostly wore classic morning suits, as he did, and the women were tastefully attired in afternoon dresses and sunhats. Later, at the evening reception, they would all change into their ballroom best.

It was only when his eyes finally found the Princess, in a small cluster of women waiting to talk to the bride, that he realised he'd been searching for her.

He cursed under his breath. His reaction to her was annoyingly primal. And annoyingly still present. The problem, he decided as he studied her, was that she had an element of the conquest about her. All that snooty standoffishness combined with her natural beauty was like a summons to any man who had red blood pumping through his veins. But while he enjoyed a challenge—possibly more than most men—some inner sense of self-preservation warned him to keep his distance.

He had very firm rules when it came to women and he never deviated from them. Keep it short, keep it sweet and, most importantly, keep it simple. This posh princess had *complicated* written all over her pretty face.

He'd seen enough relationships fall apart to last him a lifetime, and while logically he knew not all couples ended up on the scrap heap he wasn't prepared to take the chance. It was probably the only risk he wasn't willing to take, because when it all went pear-shaped the fall-out was usually devastating.

'I know that face. You're brooding about something.'

Wolfe glanced at Gilles, who had ambled up with two glasses of champagne in his hands. Wolfe took one and smiled. 'Just enjoying the frivolities.'

Gilles gave him a droll look. Previously they had both bemoaned any wedding they'd been forced to attend. 'I thought you were bringing someone with you today?'

Wolfe took a sip and tried not to wince as the warming liquid pooled in his mouth. 'Not while I'm working.'

Gilles lowered his own glass, amusement dancing in his eyes. 'She dumped you?'

Wolfe recalled the look on Astrid's angry face when he'd told her he wouldn't be seeing her again. 'Yep.'

'In…' Gilles glanced at his watch '…how many hours?'

Wolfe chuckled. He'd enjoyed Astrid's company for five busy nights while he was working in Vienna a month ago, and she had enjoyed his. When he'd tried to say goodbye she'd kicked up a stink. Accused him of using her. Wolfe's anger had surfaced then. He knew he had a name for being a heartless womaniser but he was simply honest. He didn't see the point in beating around the bush and pretending to feel things he didn't. And nor did he sleep with as many women as his reputation would suggest. He wouldn't have any time left over for work if he did.

'What can I say? She was one of the smart ones.'

Wolfe waited for his friend to start up another good-natured lecture about settling down. Anne, it seemed, had reformed the once bad-boy Marquis to the point where Wolfe now almost preferred her company to his.

'Well, that works out well for me.'

'It does?'

Gilles chuckled. 'Don't look so relieved. I wasn't about to try and reform the unreformable.'

'Thank God.'

'But I do need a favour.'

Favours Wolfe could do.

'Sure.'

'There's a girl I need you to keep your eye on tonight at the reception.'

Wolfe didn't exactly look at the sky, but he came close. 'Friend of Anne's, by chance?'

'Yes, actually. But, no, I'm not trying to set you up, you suspicious clod. She's the woman my father wanted me to marry.'

Gilles's words sparked a distant memory of a late-night chat from years back that Wolfe had completely forgotten about. He took another pull of his drink and wished it was beer in an icy bottle instead of champagne in a tepid glass. 'I'm listening.'

'Years ago my father and hers came to the decision that we would forge a strong union if we married when we came of age.'

'I think you "came of age" about ten years ago, my friend, and isn't that a little last century?'

Gilles's mouth twisted into an ironic smile. 'You've met

my father. Hers is worse. Anyway, the media have done a good job beating some life into the old story this past week, playing up the whole jilted fiancée thing, and Anne said it's been a bit rough on her.'

Wolfe knew what it felt like to be talked about behind his back. Even if the people in the small town he'd grown up in had been doing so out of sympathy rather than slander. At least for him and his brother, at any rate. 'What's wrong with her?' he asked suspiciously.

Gilles scoffed. 'Nothing. But I don't want you to sleep with her. Actually, I'd be downright angry if you did. She's gorgeous, and way too good for you. I just want you to keep an eye on her. Make sure she's having a good time.'

'Who is she?' he asked, premonition snaking down his spine.

'See the woman talking to Anne now?'

Wolfe didn't have to look to know it was the Princess from the wall and he nearly groaned. Anyone but her. But at least now it made sense why she had been so familiar with the estate. They were family friends.

Wolfe turned his back on the woman he was intent on avoiding for the rest of his life. 'I'm sure she can take care of herself.'

Gilles gave him a quizzical look and Wolfe cursed his curt tone. He had nothing against the Princess, really. Except for the fact that she'd occupied his mind all afternoon and made him want to push her sweet skirt up around her waist and take her up against the nearest hundred-year-old oak. He definitely didn't want to find out that Gilles had once been with her. Had they been lovers? The thought left a sour taste in his mouth.

'I'm sure she will, too, but as she's attending the wedding alone I thought you could keep your eye on her for me. You know—ask her to dance, make sure she has a drink.'

Today he'd been mistaken for a rescue service, a gardener

and now… 'You've got waiters for that, and I'm not a damned babysitter.'

Gilles's eyebrows shot up, but before he could say anything his new wife stepped around Wolfe and curled her arm through Gilles's. 'Babysitting who?'

Her green eyes met Wolfe's speculatively and Wolfe saw Gilles's eyes fall guiltily on someone behind him.

'I hope you do not mean me, Gilles?' Ava's tone was as lyrical and as superior as Wolfe remembered it.

Gilles stepped forward and kissed both her cheeks. 'Ava, you look as beautiful as ever.'

'I can see that you *do* mean me,' she berated lightly. 'And I can assure you I do not need babysitting.'

Her eyes briefly cut to Wolfe's with such aloof disdain it made him want to smile. He remembered her hands splayed over the ridges of his abdominal muscles as she'd clung to him on the horse. She might not like him very much, but he knew dislike wasn't the *only* emotion she felt.

'Of course you don't, *ma petite*.' Gilles humoured her. 'Now, let me introduce you to Wolfe, a good friend of mine.'

Unable to prevent himself from ruffling her regal feathers, Wolfe tilted his head. 'We've met. How's the head?' His eyes drifted to the wide-brimmed hat, tilted to one side to conceal the bruise on her forehead. The pale pink exactly matched a flirty two-piece suit that followed the line of her curves all the way to her perfectly shaped calves and slender ankles.

Exceptional legs, he thought, his gaze trekking slowly back up to her face.

She arched a brow that told him she hadn't taken kindly to his once-over, or to the implied intimacy in his tone.

'You know each other?' Gilles regarded Ava in surprise.

'No.'

'Oh?' Gilles cut his curious gaze back to Wolfe.

'Shall I tell him, or do you want to?' Wolfe drawled.

After briefly glaring all sorts of retribution his way, she

turned a serene smile on Gilles and Anne. 'It was nothing. I had a small problem with my car and your friend *kindly* provided me with a lift to the château.'

'A small problem with your car?' Gilles frowned.

Wolfe held her gaze as he felt the others turn to him and told himself to leave well enough alone. Ruffling her glorious feathers was not on his agenda, even if his body was demanding that he forge a new one—preferably starting with her naked on top of a set of silk sheets. 'What Her Highness means is that she had a car accident, climbed your outer wall and got captured by my men—'

'And stole your horse because you were being incredibly rude!' she provided, cutting Gilles's blustering in half.

Wolfe shifted his weight and stuck one hand into his pocket. 'And here I was thinking you stole him because you wanted to go for a ride.' He rubbed his hand across his abdomen, unable to stop himself from teasing her a little.

'I did think about it,' she murmured huskily, the quick dart of her pink tongue caressing her lower lip and sending a bolt of lust straight to his groin. 'But since he wasn't up to my usual standard I thought why bother?'

Wolfe laughed at her bald-faced put-down. Gilles was fortunately too worried about her accident to pick up on the subtext, but Anne's interested glances told him that she wasn't quite as obtuse.

'You weren't hurt?' Anne queried, concern lacing her words.

'A bump on the head,' Ava dismissed casually. 'Really, the whole thing was *incredibly* insignificant.'

Wolfe's lips quirked. 'You know, I wouldn't have described it that way myself.'

'No?' Ava held his gaze. 'Maybe you need to get out more.'

'Maybe I do,' he agreed, noting the line of pink that highlighted her lovely cheekbones. Maybe he needed to get out with *her*. No. He'd already decided not to go there. But, damn, he was enjoying sparring with her.

'But what were you doing on the wall?' Gilles interrupted with a frown.

'Well, trying to get down, obviously,' Ava returned pithily. 'Which would have been a lot easier if you hadn't removed that lovely old chestnut tree.'

Gilles gave a typically Gallic shrug. 'I had no choice. It was a security risk.'

Wolfe laughed right up until the moment she shared a warm smile with Gilles. Again he wondered at their history. Had she been in love with his friend? Was she still? Was that why Gilles had asked him to watch out for her? Was it possible she would cause trouble if he didn't? Questions, questions, questions. And there was really only one he wanted answered.

How responsive would she be in his bed?

His name suited him, Ava mused absently, nursing a flute of champagne as she willed the evening reception to finish.

Predatory.

Intense.

Arrogant.

And utterly transfixing when he turned those molten toffee-coloured eyes on her. Not to mention aloof and emotionally unavailable if the evening gossip was to be believed.

'They call him Ice, and apparently he has a heart as hard to find as a pink diamond,' one woman had said, giggling as she'd gazed longingly across the room at him.

Ava had rolled her eyes. She knew many women saw an unattainable man—especially a wealthy alpha male like Wolfe—as a personal challenge to go forth and rehabilitate, but she wasn't one of them. She was only interested in a man who was caring and considerate and who respected a woman as more than just a trophy to be admired and trotted out when it suited him. A gentle, sophisticated man, who was looking

for love and companionship more than short affairs with a
variety of women.

That thought reminded her of the luncheon she'd had with
Anne last month. 'Hot' and 'divine' were words that had been
bandied around when she'd talked about a friend of Gilles's
called Wolfe. As had 'confirmed bachelor'. Ava remembered
zoning out at that point, telling her friend she wasn't at all
interested in commitment-phobes like her ex. Which put
Gilles's 'hot' friend with the beautiful eyes and corrugated
abdominal muscles firmly off her Christmas list.

Even if he *did* looked incredible in a custom-made tuxedo.

Oh, stop, she scolded herself. Lots of men looked incredible in tuxedos; they were the equivalent of a corset for women.

Of course lots of men hadn't made her burn just by looking at her, or made her want to touch them all over, but that
was just bad luck. Or maybe it was more to do with how uncomfortable she felt tonight. Maybe she was just looking for a
distraction from all the polite smiles and curious stares from
many of the other guests.

Those who were friends knew that she'd never seriously
been involved with Gilles, but they were intent on having a
good time and she felt curiously lonely in the large crowd.

Her mind was intent on remembering the way Wolfe had
held her in his arms that morning, with such breathless ease
she hadn't been able to stop herself from imagining what it
would be like to kiss him. Embarrassingly, she had even held
herself perfectly still as if in anticipation of that kiss!

Pah!

She was just feeling a little strained after having to put on
a brave face all day. And, okay, she was also a little intrigued
by Wolfe. It had been a long time since a man had caught
her attention. A long time since she had wondered about his
kiss. A long time since she had felt the warmth of a man's
loving embrace. Not that Wolfe's would be loving—but it
would be warm…

Ava pulled a wry face at herself. Before today she wouldn't have said she had missed a man's embrace at all. But right now, watching this one they called Ice nonchalantly circle the room but not quite participate in the frivolities made her ache for it.

And don't try using that sexy little body to garner any favours, Princess.

Ava's lips tightened.

Arrogant.

Rude.

Unsophisticated.

Uncultured.

So why had she surreptitiously touched his body at the first opportunity?

Ava shivered and raised her champagne glass to her lips. Empty. *Drat.*

The doctor Wolfe had sent to see her—an unexpectedly nice gesture she still had to thank him for—had told her it would be best if she didn't drink tonight. Her position as 'jilted fiancée' in a room full of her peers told her it would be best if she did.

Taking another glass of Gilles's best from a passing waiter, she took a fortifying sip. It didn't surprise her that Wolfe had a reputation with women. A man who could lift a fully grown woman off a horse and lower her slowly to the ground with one hand held a certain *earthy* appeal.

For *some*, she reminded herself firmly. Not for her.

'My dance, I believe?'

For a minute Ava imagined the deep voice behind her was Wolfe, but it lacked a certain velvety-rough tenor and hadn't sent any delicious tingles down her spine so she knew it wasn't. Turning, she smiled at a nice English Lord who had been hounding her all night.

She didn't feel like dancing with him, but nor did she feel like triggering more gossip by refusing every man who approached her. Smiling with a polite reserve she hoped he read as, *Lovely, but be assured I'm not interested in furthering our acquaintance*, she stepped into his arms. Which was when she caught sight of Wolfe, watching her yet again from across the room. Her eyes immediately ran over the woman at his side, who looked young, happy and relaxed. By contrast Ava felt old, surly and uptight. Which was partly Wolfe's fault, she thought churlishly, because she couldn't seem to stop thinking about him.

And the fact that he had a beautiful woman at his side while he held his eyes on her only confirmed that the talk about him playing the field was true. Unless he had been watching her all night because of Gilles's silly request that he 'babysit' her. For some reason the latter thought aggravated Ava more than the former.

Five minutes later, feeling as graceful as a goose under Wolfe's constant regard, she sent her dance partner to fetch her a glass of water so she could find out. She didn't need an audience when she told Wolfe that his attention was not only supremely annoying but totally unnecessary.

Orientating herself in the vast room, she located him lazily propping up a wall in a dimly lit section of the ballroom, feeling ridiculously elated when she found the bubbly blonde was no longer running her fingernails up and down his powerful forearm.

He didn't say anything when she stopped in front of him, just looked down at her through a screen of thick dark lashes that made his mood impossible to gauge. Not that it mattered. She was here about *her* feelings, not his.

'You are eyeing me off because Gilles asked you, too, no?' She knew she'd mixed up her words—her English was always clumsy when she was agitated.

'I think the term you're looking for is *watching over you*.'

Amusement laced his tone and her spine stiffened in annoyance.

'I don't need watching.'

'I thought all women liked to be watched. Isn't that why you wrap yourselves up in those slinky dresses?' His drink swayed as he made an up-and-down motion with his hand.

Ava glanced down at her strapless jade-green gown, which was fitted to the waist and then fell to the floor in silky waves. 'My dress is elegant, not *slinky*.'

'Why don't we agree on elegantly slinky, for argument's sake?'

He was smooth, this handsome Australian, very smooth. 'I do not need babysitting,' Ava said, reminding herself that she had not approached him to flirt with him.

'I never said you did. In fact I told Gilles you could take care of yourself.'

'Presumably because I made off with your horse?'

'You didn't make off with my horse.' The pitch of his voice dropped subtly. 'But you did play a pretty dangerous game on him.'

Ava's heart kicked up a notch at his silky taunt. 'I'm quite sure I don't know what you mean.'

Wolfe smiled. 'I'm quite sure you do.'

He took a lazy sip of his beer and her eyes were drawn to the strong column of his throat when he swallowed. She looked up to find that his eyes had closed to half-mast as she watched him and her breasts grew heavy.

Determined to ignore the sensation, she continued. 'So, if you are not doing Gilles's bidding, why do you watch me?'

'Why do you think?'

His eyes toured over her body and she had a pretty good indication of why. Something hot and quivery vibrated up and down her spine. The memory of the feel of his hands on her torso returned. They were so large they had almost swallowed her whole.

Perturbed by the physical response he so effortlessly created in her, Ava shook her head. Compared to her he appeared so cool and relaxed, and yet she was sure if she touched him he'd feel as tightly coiled as a spring.

'I think you are a man who gets what he wants a little too often, Ice!' she challenged, deciding that he was messing with her head. The way he looked at her. The way his eyes lingered on her mouth. She knew he felt the chemistry between them and she wondered why she wanted to push him to show her. Even more she wondered what it would take to make this self-contained man lose control.

'Is that so?'

'Yes.' Ava tried to match his careless tone even though her heart was thumping inside her chest. 'The word in the powder room is that you steal hearts wherever you go.'

'Have you been talking about me, Princess?'

Ava felt her temper spike at his evasiveness. 'That's not an answer.'

His eyebrow rose at her sharp tone. 'You didn't ask a question.'

Wanting to stamp her foot in frustration, she decided the smart thing to do was to bid him goodnight. She'd already decided to ignore the way he made her feel, and yet here she was almost begging him to make her change her mind.

Dragging her eyes from his sensual half smile, she took a step back and curled a stray wisp of hair behind her ear. 'Fine. If you'll—'

His hand shot out and snagged her upper arm. His hold was gentle, yet uncompromising, and she couldn't prevent a gasp of surprise at the unexpectedness of it. 'Don't play games with me, Rapunzel. I guarantee you'll lose.'

Ava barely contained her temper. If anyone was playing games here it was him, not her. And if a small voice in her head was asking her if trying to get the better of him on the lawn earlier had not been a game—well, she didn't much care right now.

'You have that wrong.' She lifted her chin. 'I am not the

one playing games here.' Because deep down she knew it would be beyond stupid to invite this man into her life in any capacity.

He stared at her, finally letting the sensual heat she had felt in him all night shine through in his eyes. She couldn't look away, like a deer caught in headlights as he inexorably drew closer—only realising it was she who had swayed towards him when a glass of mineral water was thrust in front of her face.

'There you are,' Lord Parker puffed, pushing his chest out in Wolfe's direction.

Half expecting Wolfe to challenge him, Ava was absurdly disappointed when all he did was slide a thumb across the rampaging pulse-point in her wrist before releasing her. As if as an afterthought he bent towards her, his mouth close to her ear, his intoxicating scent making her breathless.

'Careful what you wish for, Princess. You just might get it.' He straightened and inclined his head in her direction. 'If you'll excuse me?' He mimicked the cool words she'd been about to serve him moments earlier before striding across the marble floor and into another room.

Ava let out a long pent-up breath. She should be glad he was gone. He was arrogant, obnoxious, and too cool for school—and yet he made her burn hotter than any man ever had before. It was a powerful aphrodisiac. All-consuming and tempting. And despite the fact that he had just warned her off some obtuse part of her still wanted to know what it would feel like to have those capable hands on her heated skin—her *naked*, heated skin.

'Ladies and gentlemen…'

The MC interrupted Ava's conflicting thoughts.

'The bride is about to throw her bouquet before the couple departs for the evening.'

A triumphant squeal rent the air as the bouquet was caught by one of Anne's American friends, followed by a stream of synchronised clapping as the bride and groom made their way upstairs. They would be spending the night at the château before leaving for their honeymoon after luncheon the following day.

Ava joined in the well-wishing but her chest felt tight. Anne and Gilles were so happy. So in love. An old fear that she would never get to experience that depth of emotion with someone special cut across the happiness she felt for them both.

Realising she must be more out of balance than she'd first thought, she decided to call it a night. Glancing around the room, she noted that Wolfe was nowhere to be seen and felt another stab of irritation at herself. She was torn between wanting him to want her and wanting him not to. It was as if she was somehow in thrall to him. As if her brain no longer functioned, or it functioned but was stuck in one groove, like the needle on an old-fashioned record player. The word *sex* was going round and round in her head like an endlessly exciting mantra.

Ava stared at her water glass and wondered if someone had drugged it. The last thing she wanted was sex with a man completely unsuitable for her hopes and dreams. Wasn't it?

Annoyed, she pivoted on her heel—and gasped when she nearly ran smack into the man who had occupied her mind pretty much the entire day and night.

'You're leaving before our dance,' he murmured silkily.

The balls of her feet hurt and she didn't want to dance. 'I did not think you played games.' She could barely hear her own voice above the sound of her thundering heartbeat. Had he been toying with her to heighten her awareness of him? If so, it had worked. She had never been more aware of a man in her life.

She saw his nostrils flare at her confrontational tone and something primal unfurled low in her pelvis, because she knew that he *did* play games. And even though it went against

all her principles part of her wanted to play—with him—
tonight.

'Maybe I want to feel you in my arms one more time.'

Heat rushed through her body as his husky words burned
her up inside. *How did any woman stop herself from drowning under such blazingly sexual intensity?*

'Do you?'

As if sensing her near capitulation, he gave her a lupine
smile. 'Yes.' He set her drink aside and swept her into his
arms.

Ava's stomach flipped. She'd like to think that she'd *let*
him walk her backwards onto the dance floor—although that
would imply she still had some influence over her actions and
she wasn't sure that she did.

'What about what *I* want?' The question was meant to establish some sense of control on her part, but she suspected
that he knew what he did to her and had seen right through it.

He brought the hand holding hers towards her face and ro-
tated it so that his knuckles gently drifted across her cheek-
bone. 'This *is* what you want, Princess.'

A cascade of sensations made her shiver and she told herself to tread carefully. Told herself that there was only one
kind of man who parried around a woman all night and then
approached her at the end. The kind her mother would have
told her to steer well clear of. What it said about her wanting
him regardless she didn't want to think about.

He was so sure. So confident. She should shoot him down
in flames. Using his own pistol to do it.

Instead she braced herself against his magnetic sensuality
and told herself she would walk away at the end of the song.

'One dance.'

CHAPTER THREE

DANCE? WOLFE DIDN'T want to dance with her. He wanted to possess her. And for a self-confessed non-game-player he had played a game of parry and retreat with her to rival all others.

Not intentionally.

His *intention* had been to avoid her. But once she'd entered the ballroom in a green dress that flowed around her body like a caressing hand he'd been lost.

Well, maybe not lost. More like mesmerised. And it had annoyed the hell out of him that he'd noticed that every other male in the room felt the same way. The married ones couldn't do anything about it, but the single ones had been lining up as if she was a participant in some secret speed-dating service.

He, on the other hand, had spent most of the night fighting the urge to muscle his way through the throng of wedding guests and throw her over his shoulder like the barbarian she had accused him of being. Hell, his body had been so attuned to hers he'd practically known every time she'd blinked.

Chemistry. He'd never experienced it quite so strongly. But he knew the quickest way to appease it would be to have her. So far he'd steadfastly stuck to his plan not to go near her but, hell, why not? He was only responding to her like any other healthy male who had held a beautiful woman in his arms and wanted her. Nothing complicated about that.

In fact it was so simple he didn't know why he was dwelling on it so much.

He would have had more to dwell on if he *hadn't* wanted her. And as for that instant tilting of the world he'd felt earlier when he'd caught her…well, it was only lust. Raw, pagan, blow-your-head-open lust. Perfectly rational. Perfectly normal.

Wolfe looked down into her face. Her cheeks were pink and her lips were softly parted as she breathed shallowly. His gaze drifted lower, to the firm thrust of her breasts, her aroused nipples, and then back up. Her gaze was slumberous but slightly guarded, as if she too were a little taken aback by the strength of this thing between them.

Without making a conscious decision to do so, he spread his hand possessively over her hip, pressing her closer. He knew the minute she felt his hardness because she made one of those softly feminine sounds that had his body jerking in response.

It made him want to spear his hand in her upswept hair and drag her mouth to his, but at the last minute the sounds of the party still in progress penetrated his desire-drugged mind. Instead he cupped her chin in his palm and brought her eyes to his. 'I want you, Ava. I want to kiss you until you can't see straight and make love to you until you can't move. I've thought of nothing else all day.'

A shiver raced through her and Wolfe felt as if he was poised on the blade of a knife as he waited for her response.

'I…' She blew out a breath. Swallowed heavily. 'Okay.'

Exalted, and no longer questioning his need for her, Wolfe grabbed her hand and fought to keep his steps measured as he led her off the dance floor.

She'd been allocated a room in the east wing of the château and he didn't pause for breath until, on the second-floor landing, he felt a soft tug on his hand.

Turning, he watched her run her hands down the sides of her dress, the nervous gesture only serving to mould it closer. 'Wolfe.' She cleared her throat. 'I'm not sure this is such a good idea.'

Wolfe wasn't sure about anything except that the sound of his name in her husky, accented voice twisted his insides into a mess. A very hot mess. 'Not sure what is such a good idea? This?'

He backed her against the stone wall and raised his hands to frame her face. Then he used every ounce of skill he possessed and leant down to claim her mouth with his.

Immediately his senses became overloaded with the rich, intoxicating taste of her. He'd known it would be like this. Overpowering. Overwhelming. Her ruby lips were so much fuller and sweeter than he had imagined, and when she parted them and pressed closer the instinct to ravage her consumed him.

His fingers dug into her scalp to hold her steady as he deepened the kiss, his tongue sweeping into her mouth to explore every corner.

'Wolfe, please...'

Her soft whimper of need inflamed him to the point of madness. He couldn't get enough of her. His hands shaped her slender curves, desperate to delve under the dress, and he was keenly satisfied when she ardently returned his hunger. Her uncertainty of moments ago was flung into the flames of a desire so bright it burned him alive.

She was sensational, and he ground himself against her in ardent anticipation. He couldn't remember ever feeling this frenzy of need before, and it was just dumb luck that a door banged somewhere along the corridor and brought him back to his senses.

Fighting for control, he grabbed her hand again and didn't stop until they were both breathless and inside her bedroom, the door firmly closed behind.

He hit the light switch and stared at her.

She stood in the centre of the historically preserved room like a pagan offering, her lips already moist and swollen from his kisses. She sucked in a deep breath and he thought he saw a shadow of vulnerability chase itself across her face.

It gave him a moment's pause.

He had avoided thinking about a woman in any serious capacity his whole life, after having to clean up the damage his mother had caused by her actions. But this wasn't serious. Making love—having sex, he amended—with Ava de Veers was not a threat to his wellbeing in any way, shape or form.

It was about pleasure. Mutual, unadulterated pleasure.

'I like the light on,' he rasped.

She moistened her lips. 'I don't…mind.'

Satisfied that he knew exactly what he was doing, Wolfe shoved away from the door and paced towards her. He stopped a breath from touching her and gazed into her wide-spaced smoky eyes, searching out any further signs of apprehension, promising himself he would stop if she showed even a hint of uncertainty. Fortunately he didn't have to test that theory, because her gaze could have melted iron when it met his.

His iron will.

Shaking off the insidious devil of doubt that told him once was never going to be enough with this woman, he curled one hand around the nape of her neck and pulled her up onto her toes. She steadied herself by placing her hands on his shoulders. The air between them turned to syrup as she tilted her head back into his hand, presenting him with the elegant arch of her neck.

Wolfe felt his lip curl upward as he thought of the recent vampire craze in the cinemas. Suddenly he understood the draw. Lust pounded through his blood and he brought his other hand up to trace the tender skin she had exposed to his hungry gaze. She opened her eyes, stared into his, and then did something he hadn't expected—she took charge and pressed her lips to his.

He let her sip and nibble at his mouth for maybe ten seconds before that primal feeling she dredged up in him took over. Then his hands and lips firmed and he forced her mouth wide, demanding that she cede everything to him.

And she did. Without hesitation. Her slender arms snaking behind his neck, her body arching into his.

Wolfe told himself to ease off before he scared both of them, but her mouth angled more comfortably under his and he didn't know how it was possible but she took the kiss deeper. Wrapped her sweet tongue around his and made his head spin.

Without really being aware of his surroundings he wrenched his jacket off and pushed her fumbling fingers aside to tear at the buttons on his shirt. Shucking out of it, he welcomed the bite of cooler air on his overheated flesh and the layer of sensation it added.

He released the dark mane of her hair from its tight coil and felt his heart wrench as it cascaded past her delicate shoulders.

Ignoring the swirling emotions ebbing and flowing through his mind, he cupped her breasts and moulded them in his hands. Soft and round, the nipples already poking through the silky fabric of her dress like tiny diamonds. He kneaded and shaped her, his eyes on her face as he roughly dragged his thumbs across both her nipples at once.

'Oh, Wolfe. *Mon Dieu.*'

Her husky groan urged him to draw the hidden side-zipper of her dress down until her pale, perfect breasts stood proud and taut in front of him.

'Ava, you're—' He swore as words failed him and bent to draw a dusky pink nipple into his starving mouth. The taste of her made him throb, and when she clutched his head to hold him closer he gave up any pretense of finesse, scooping her into his arms and yanking off the ugly floral bedspread before depositing her on crisp white sheets.

She leant up on her elbows and watched him through heavy-lidded eyes as he dragged the silky gown from her long legs and tossed it aside.

Wolfe took her in as he stripped off his remaining clothing: her wavy hair a dark ripple down her back, her sweet breasts rising and falling in time with her heavy breaths, her narrow waist, and the sheer purple panties that revealed more than they hid.

Her woman's scent rose up to tease him and he climbed onto the bed and came over her, his hands braced on either side of her face. 'Now, my lovely, I have you right where I want you.'

Her hands came up between them, curling into his chest hair. Her smile was full of womanly provocation. Her actions thankfully belying her earlier hesitation. 'You like to think you're in control, but I am stronger than I look.' She scratched her nails lightly against his skin like a cat.

She shuddered beautifully beneath him and turned her head to capture his mouth with hers. He groaned, sank into the kiss, let himself become absorbed by it. His free hand smoothed down over her torso, learning her wherever he went.

Her own hands were busy, stroking up over the muscles of his arms. When she pushed playfully against his shoulders he didn't budge. 'It feels like you're made of steel. You're completely immovable.'

'Where do you want me to go?' he growled with husky promise. 'Up?' He kissed his way along her neck and bit down gently on her earlobe. 'Or down?' His tongue laved her collarbone and dipped lower, circling ever closer to the centre of her breast.

Her eyes glazed over with desire.

'Ava?'

'Quoi?' She arched off the bed, her breasts begging for his mouth.

'Which way?'

She gave a low moan as he continued to tease her, and when she wrapped one leg around his lean hip he guessed her intention and let her flip him onto his back. She pushed up until she straddled his waist. 'Now who's got whom exactly where they want them?' she said, a look of triumph lighting up her face.

Wolfe grinned and repositioned her until her hot centre cradled his erection. 'That would be me.'

'Ohhh.' Ava spread her palms wide over his chest. 'I know you think—'

Wolfe leant up and suckled one of her peaked nipples into his mouth, cutting off whatever she was about to say. Her wet heat was shredding his control and the time for banter was well past. 'I think you're sensational.' He switched to her other breast and realised that he meant it.

Usually a woman was content to let him lead all the play in bed, but this was much more fun. And the taste of her cherry-red nipples blew his mind.

While she was distracted by his mouth he smoothed his hand down her belly and cupped her where she was open and already wet for him, her filmy panties no barrier to his questing fingers. Her eyes flew open as he found her and pushed a finger inside her slick centre. She cried out his name and balanced over him as she rocked against his hand.

Wolfe's erection jerked painfully but he forced himself to wait, enjoying having her at his mercy. Enjoying the astonished look of pleasure that came over her when he lightly circled her clitoris. And especially enjoying the way she flung her head back in ecstasy and screamed his name as she came for him.

He rode out her orgasm with her until her head flopped

forward, her long hair falling around his face like a silky veil. Needing to be inside her with an urgency that was shocking, Wolfe flipped her onto her back, chuckling softly when she just lay there in silent supplication.

'At least I know how to get your absolute cooperation now.'

Ava pushed her hair back from her face and stretched sinuously. 'What did you just do to me?'

'I made you come.' He rolled on the condom he'd pulled from his wallet and nudged her thighs wider, entering her on one slow, luxurious thrust. 'And now I'm going to do it all over again.'

It took every ounce of control he possessed to keep his movements even and gentle until her body had grown accustomed to his size, but when he felt her completely relax and take all of him fully he couldn't hold back, driving them both to the edge of reason a number of times, until with a sob she gripped his hips and forced him over the edge into a space that was so white-hot he felt as if their bodies would be fused for eternity.

His last coherent thought was, what did he do after an experience like that?

With sexual release came clarity, and Ava could barely believe what had just happened. Had she *really* just had sex with a man she'd met merely hours ago? A friend of Gilles's, no less?

Yes, she had. The evidence was still there in the tiny aftershocks of pleasure rippling through her core, not to mention the harsh breaths of the man lying beside her who looked as if he was choosing his best exit line.

She made a small sound in the back of her throat. 'I told myself I wasn't going to give in to this.'

Her voice had him rolling towards her and the bed dipped under his powerful frame. Ava's skin burned where his eyes raked over her, and as casually as she could she pulled the top sheet up to cover her nudity.

'Why did you?' His voice was gravelly. Sexy.

Was that a serious question? She'd done it because at the time she'd felt she didn't have a choice. As soon as he'd taken her into his arms she hadn't been able to help herself.

'Curiosity,' she said, the word sounding much better to her ears than, *I couldn't help myself.*

'That sounds a bit calculated.' His eyes narrowed as if he was assessing her. Judging her.

'Hardly.' Did he think she had set out to sleep with him?

Embarrassed by the thought, Ava wondered what happened now. Did they engage in polite conversation? Did he get up and leave? Well, he had to, because this was her room, but…

Unsure of herself, and hating the way that made her feel—as if she was standing in front of her father about to be told off for not living up to his expectations—she decided that she had no choice but to fall back on her usual tricks of feigned indifference or taking charge. Since indifference seemed too far out of her reach right now, she chose the latter.

'Please do not feel like you have to stay around because of me. You must be tired, and I'm not the sensitive type.'

Wolfe propped his hand on his elbow, a lazy smile curling his lips. 'This is your idea of pillow-talk?'

No. It was her idea of self-defence. She feigned a yawn. 'Or if you're not tired, I am.'

His golden-brown eyes grew flinty. 'Are you asking me to leave or telling me?'

'Isn't that what you were just thinking you should do?'

His eyes flickered from hers for the briefest of seconds, but it was enough for her to know she had been right in her assumption.

'Actually, I was thinking of inviting you out to dinner.'

His comment took her by surprise, and she was sure he was making it up. She swallowed heavily and pushed aside the tiny kernel of pleasure his words had imbued her with. 'I'd love to, but you're about five hours too late.'

He shook his head in amusement. 'Are you always this prickly after a bout of hot sex?'

Ava swallowed. She didn't know. She'd never had sex like that before. The whole thing both alarmed her and set her body on fire in equal measure. What had happened to her promise only to go out with men who wanted the same thing she did? Love. A family.

Hating the feeling of uncertainty that had her in its tight grip, and hoping she appeared as casual as Wolfe, she let her eyes drift over his stubbled jaw and broad shoulders. When she noticed a small patch of puckered skin right beneath his collarbone she frowned.

'That was a bullet from a semi-automatic.'

Ava's startled gaze met his. Was he serious?

He'd said it as if he was ordering a sandwich from a deli.

'Ouch!' Keeping her voice light to match his as she noticed another scar lower down, she said, 'And this?'

He wrapped a lock of her hair around his finger and started to play with it. 'Shrapnel.'

She pointed to another small mark on his arm. 'Spurned lover?' she queried flippantly, understanding on some level that these wounds weren't badges of honour for him, but represented the deep pain and suffering brought by the uglier side of the life he had once led.

'Accurate sniper.'

He brushed the ends of her hair across her upper chest, where the sheet stopped. Ava felt goose bumps shimmer across her skin and hoped he didn't notice.

'I take it you're not very good at your job?' she teased.

His eyes glittered with amusement. 'That's one way of looking at it.' He let go of her hair and replaced it with his fingers, his movements causing the fabric to drag across her sensitised breasts.

Anticipation made her body throb and, powerless to stop herself, she let her eyes drift lower, taking in the thin trail of hair that bisected his ripped abdomen and moving down towards the magnificent erection rising straight out from his body—which was when she saw a jagged white scar that ran along his outer hip towards his thigh.

Her attention torn between the two, she was only vaguely aware of him chuckling. 'You sure you want to know about that one?'

'The scar?'

'That, too,' he teased.

She shook her head. 'What happened?'

'An unfortunate rendezvous with a piece of barbed wire, thanks to one ferociously competitive younger brother. Not very glamorous.'

'Glamorous!' Her brows drew together. 'None of them are *glamorous*!'

'You'd be surprised how many women find them a turn-on.'

She shuddered. 'I don't.'

'No?' He touched her face almost reverently, gently stroking around the bump on her head that—thankfully—pain-killers had taken care of.

Ava smiled and again surprised herself by touching her lips to his. Something flickered in his darkened eyes as she pulled back. It was some unnamed emotion, and the air between them seemed to pulse. She saw the instant Wolfe rejected whatever it was he was feeling and then, in a move that startled with its swiftness, she found herself flat on her back, with him once again braced over the top of her. He captured her hands in one of his and raised them above her head, the completely carnal smile on his lips making her heartbeat quicken.

'Wolfe, we probably shouldn't do this again,' Ava breathed, wishing there was a little more conviction behind her words.

Wolfe lowered his mouth to hers and nudged her thighs further apart with his knees, grabbed his last condom and slipped inside her wet, welcoming heat. 'We probably shouldn't have done it in the first place,' he said on a long groan.

CHAPTER FOUR

WOLFE SCOWLED AS he marched across the circular driveway of the château towards the outer cottage, the quartz driveway crunching loudly beneath his boots in the morning air. It was still early, the sky etched in palest blue with a ribbon of orange rimming the horizon.

Why the hell had he invited her to dinner? And would she take it to mean tonight?

He wasn't even meant to be in town tonight. He had a huge meeting first thing tomorrow morning in Hamburg. He didn't have time to wine and dine a woman. So he'd tell her. Apologise. Explain that he'd forgotten about the business meeting.

He winced inwardly. She'd no doubt think it was an excuse...but what else could he do?

An image of waking up beside her caused him to clench his jaw. After years of practice his body had clicked on just before dawn, and he'd come instantly awake to find a warm, sexy woman curled into his side, with her head cushioned on his numb shoulder and her hand curled over his heart, the soft skin of her upper back silky smooth beneath his rough hands.

No.

There was no way he could have dinner with her—tonight or any other night. The sex had been great—more than great—but he rarely visited Paris, and even if he did he'd have very little time to see her again. And the last thing he needed was another ear-bashing from a woman who wanted more than he could give.

Would Ava be like that? Start accusing him of using her even though they'd both agreed on short-term? He didn't know. And then he almost missed a step as he realised that he and Ava hadn't agreed on anything last night. They'd been too busy ripping each other's clothes off.

Wolfe grinned. Blew out a short breath. Last night had been something else. *She* had been something else. Hot beneath all that regal perfection. He knew if Gilles found out he'd slept with her he'd hop into him, but… His smile turned to a frown. Had Gilles ever held her so intimately? Come to think of it, had *he* ever held a woman so intimately after sex? Didn't he sleep on his stomach as a general rule?

No.

Entering into an affair with his friend's ex-fiancée wasn't going to work for either of them. Better to nip it in the bud now. Tell her it had been wonderful—more wonderful than he'd had in… What did that matter? It had been great. She had been great. But they were adults whose lives were vastly different.

Hell.

He stopped with his hand on the cottage doorknob.

He *had* to take her out to dinner. He might not have been one hundred percent truthful when he'd told her he had been thinking about asking her last night, but he wasn't a complete bastard. The least he could do after the night they'd shared was take her out for a meal.

So, okay, they'd go out. He'd choose a nice little out-of-the-way restaurant, make her feel special, take her home, maybe finish the night off with more sex—not that *that* was a deal-breaker—then he'd leave and his world would be right again.

Nice and simple. Job done.

He turned the knob and greeted his men as he entered the

cottage, not at all sure whether he should be bothered by the unusual level of excitement he felt at the thought of seeing her again.

Ava woke alone and realised immediately from the heat in the room that it was late. Then memory kicked in, facilitated by the lingering scent of Wolfe on the other pillow and the fact that she was naked.

She didn't know what had possessed her to sleep with him last night, but she knew she had definitely not been thinking with her head screwed on straight. No way would she have done all those things if it had been. No way would she have given herself so completely to a man she hardly knew if… A wicked thrill raced through her as images of Wolfe's magnificent body filtered through her mind and she frowned. She wasn't into cavemen, no matter how charismatic, and she had never been one to drool over a gorgeous face and body.

Before, a little voice chirped annoyingly.

Ever, Ava countered decisively.

She pushed her hair back from her face and smoothed out some of the knots caused by Wolfe's warm fingers. Her core pulsed with remembered pleasure and she groaned at her body's willingness to relive every erotic moment. Yes, there was definitely something to be said about all the dips and bulges of warm, sold muscle, and the man certainly knew his way around the female body. But so he should. According to Anne, he had enough experience for ten men. And she didn't have time in her life for someone like that. She was over shallow hook-ups where the male wanted sex and the female wanted a relationship.

Last night had been… Last night had been sensational, yes. But it was an aberration. One of those things out of the box that you couldn't quite explain but you knew you probably shouldn't have done. Too much champagne, too much anxiety about being at the wedding, too much overpowering testosterone in the form of one blond, godlike male.

Jumping out of bed to distract herself, Ava winced as long-unused muscles registered all that godlike male possession. He was just so big. So strong. When he'd manacled her hands and held her prisoner... Ava shivered and rejected her body's instant softening. But he'd just played with her and then he'd left. His actions spoke more loudly than his words ever could.

That old insecurity she'd thought long gone raised its knobbly head like a sleepy dragon and yawned. But she wouldn't go there. She'd dealt with that childish feeling when she'd moved to Paris, and it was no longer relevant to who she was now.

Maybe this whole business—her father's phone call combined with her emotional response to the wedding—had affected her more than she'd allowed herself to consider, made her act out of character.

Another one of Anne's comments snuck into her consciousness. 'Women drop like lemmings around him,' she'd said at lunch. 'But he lives a fast-paced life. According to Gilles, the man is never in the same city for longer than a few days at a time. It's like he's combing the globe for some holy grail.'

More like variety in his bed, Ava thought with a burst of asperity. And good luck to him. She hoped he enjoyed himself.

He did invite you to dinner, that devil's voice reminded her.

Yes, out of some sort of guilt, she told herself. He'd sensed her uneasiness after the sex and had made the invitation on the spur of the moment. It had been a nice gesture but his voice had lacked conviction. And his actions this morning only backed that up.

No.

She wouldn't be having dinner with Wolfe. He didn't really want to take her out and it would only be prolonging the inevitable. Also, she could think of nothing worse than forcing someone to do something they didn't want to do. That was her father's *modus operandi*, not hers.

Okay.

Shower. Get dressed. Hire a car. Drive back to Paris. She had a meeting with a new artist she was sure was going to be a pain in the backside but who had the potential of van Gogh and she couldn't be late.

She didn't have time to dwell on a man who had taken as much pleasure as she had without any promises for the future.

When the right one came along she would know it, and until then—well, she was nearly thirty. She didn't have time to waste time on casual encounters with ripped Australian security experts. And if fate was kinder than it had been yesterday she wouldn't run into him this morning and would be spared the whole awkward morning-after thing.

Feeling more like her normal self after a shower, she smiled as she crossed the marble foyer and propped her small suitcase beside the front door. Bending down, she'd retrieved the thank-you note she'd written to Anne and Gilles, which she planned to leave with Gilles's butler, when she heard a dark voice behind her.

'Leaving so soon?'

Ava wheeled around, her hair flying over her shoulders in a slow arc. Wolfe stood in the arched doorway, ruggedly handsome in worn boots, black low-riding denims and a basic white T-shirt that drew her eye to every solid inch of him.

Placing her hand against her chest, Ava tried to smile into his hard face. 'You scared me.'

He crossed his arms over his chest. 'Obviously.'

'I…ah…' God, she sounded like a silly debutante! And why did he look so angry all of a sudden? It wasn't as if she had been the one to walk out on *him* before the birds had started chirping. 'I have a busy day lined up.'

* * *

Wolfe could tell instantly that Ava had put last night behind her. It was in the regal tilt of her head, the squared shoulders and the way her gaze didn't quite meet his. Not to mention the small, reserved smile she bestowed on him, as if all that had passed between them last night had been polite conversation instead of intimate body fluids. It was the same smile he'd seen her give plenty of other men the night before, and to say he felt infuriated by it would be a grand understatement.

He recalled the way she'd told him he could leave her room after sex. At the time he'd thought she had been politely trying to *give* him an out, but what if she'd been trying to *get* him out instead?

'On a Sunday?'

Her chin came up, most likely because of his sceptical tone. 'Yes.'

'And what about dinner?' he asked casually.

It appeared she had a guilty conscience, because her gaze cut to the left before returning to his. 'Tonight?'

Damn.

Wolfe read her meaning in that single word and knew she had no intention of having dinner with him, that night or any other. He didn't like it. 'Yeah. You, me, a bottle of red. Or do you prefer champagne?'

'Actually, I have a meeting with someone this afternoon, so I won't be able to make tonight.'

Someone she was sleeping with, perhaps?

Wolfe raked her slender figure in a floaty summer dress and lightweight sandals and tried to rein in his uncharacteristically possessive response as his mind immediately stripped her naked.

On some level he knew he was behaving completely irrationally. Really, he should be rejoicing that she didn't want to complicate things between them by prolonging the inevitable, because—well…he knew his interest in her would wane at some point.

'And it's probably better this way, don't you think?' she said a little too quickly.

'Better what way?' He refolded his arms and rocked back on his heels. No way would he make this easy for her.

Her gaze snapped irritably to his and then cast over him, lighting little bushfires in its wake. 'Better if we forget dinner. Forget last night.'

'Forget last night?' Wolfe wasn't sure if this had ever happened to him before. A woman waking up after a night of phenomenal sex who not only didn't want to have dinner with him but looked as if she never wanted to see him again either.

'Oh, come on, Wolfe.' Her slender hands fitted around her hips just as his had done last night. 'I'm sure this isn't a novel concept for you. In fact it's probably a relief.'

His eyes rose to hers as he forced himself to focus. A relief? Yes, it *should* have felt like a damned relief. The fact that it felt more like an insult only increased his aggravation.

'You think I pick women up and sleep with them every time I go out?'

'I don't know.'

And she didn't care, if he read her tone correctly.

'But why are we arguing? Did you want more from last night than just sex?'

He stiffened, suddenly uncomfortable as she turned the tables on him. Saying no just felt wrong, but… 'No.'

She nodded quickly, as if she'd expected his answer. Wanted it, in fact. Did *she* do this all the time? Pick up men for a night of no-strings sex? The idea made his stomach knot.

'Great, so we're on the same page. Last night was lovely. I had a good time. Hopefully you did, too.'

She shrugged almost apologetically and he had an unpleasant moment of wondering if this was how women felt when he walked away from them. But then with all the previous women in his life he'd established the parameters from the start. Perhaps he was just reacting badly because this time he hadn't done that.

'What more is there to say?'

Ava's challenging question brought his mind back to her.

'Clearly nothing,' Wolfe ground out. 'You seem to have it all worked out.'

She mashed her lips together, as if confused by his tone, and Wolfe warned himself to stop being stupid. This was the perfect scenario, wasn't it?

The sound of footsteps coming down the grand staircase drew his eye, and then he heard Ava swear in French.

'Gilles is coming. I don't want… Can we just pretend this never happened?' She tinkled a laugh. 'Yes, the wedding was gor— Oh, Gilles. *Bonjour*. Where's Anne?'

Wolfe thought about telling her never to try her hand at acting. She looked as innocent as someone trying to make off with the family jewels.

He narrowed his eyes as Gilles put his hands on her waist and gave her a kiss on each cheek, disturbed by the unexpected urge to pull him off her.

'As quaint as Anne finds the ancient staff bell in our room, it didn't work this morning—so I've been sent in search of coffee.'

'What a fantastic idea.' Ava nodded enthusiastically. 'I think I might join you.'

'You want one, Wolfe?' Gilles rubbed his eyes, as if he hadn't had much sleep.

Wolfe knew how he felt.

'No. I've had enough coffee to last me a lifetime.' Ava's pout firmed, and Gilles threw him a quizzical look.

Deciding it was past time he left, he shoved his hand into his pocket for his keys and felt the phone he'd put there to give to Ava.

'This is for you.' He held out a silver smartphone. 'I took

the liberty of placing your SIM card into a spare after my men found yours broken in your car.'

'Oh.' She looked confused by the gesture. 'You didn't have to do that.'

He knew he didn't. He'd wanted to.

He turned it on and passed it to her, before informing Gilles of his plans to hit the road earlier than he'd intended.

While Gilles tried to convince him to reconsider, Ava's phone beeped a string of incoming messages. They both turned to see her frowning at it.

Wolfe immediately felt his guard go up. 'What's wrong?'

'My father has left ten messages. Excuse me while I retrieve them.'

She dialled a number and pressed the phone to her ear at the same time as Gilles's butler hurried into the foyer.

Momentarily distracted when he handed Gilles a piece of paper, Wolfe returned his gaze to Ava in time to see the colour leach out of her face.

She turned almost blindly to Gilles, her breathing erratic. 'Frédéric has been involved in an accident. Gilles…' Her voice trailed off when Gilles looked at her, and if possible she lost even more colour. *'Quoi?'*

Wolfe didn't think she'd realised that she had reached out and was gripping his forearm in a talonlike hold.

Gilles shook his head as if in a daze.

Hell.

'I need to speak with my father. Find out what hospital he is in.' Ava's shaky hands fumbled with the phone, and it would have dropped if Wolfe hadn't swiftly bent to catch it.

'Ava, he's not in hospital.'

'Ne sois pas absurde, Gilles. The accident sounds serious.' She shook her head, unable to say more.

Wolfe cursed under his breath.

'Ava—'

'No.' She held up her hand and cut him off, backing away

from both of them, so disorientated she would have bumped into the wall if Wolfe hadn't reached out and grabbed her by the elbows.

'Breathe, Ava,' he instructed levelly. 'In. Out. That's it.'

Her gaze cleared a little and her body went rigid as she pushed his hand away. 'I'm fine.'

Wolfe's mouth tightened. 'Give me the phone,' he ordered. 'I'll call your father.'

She swallowed heavily, her navy eyes bruised. He would have wrapped his arms around her then, pulled her in close, but she was so rigid she might as well have been wearing armour. He'd thought he'd sensed fragility in her—the same as he'd sensed last night—but if he had it was long gone.

Ignoring the voice in his head that told him he should butt out of her affairs and mind his own business, he scrolled through her phone. When he couldn't find an entry under 'Dad' or 'Father' he glanced at her. 'What's his name?'

'It's listed under "The Tyrant".'

Her chin came up, as if defying him to make a comment; the action told him that the moniker hadn't been given in jest. But was her father really a tyrant? Or was she just another spoilt little girl who threw tantrums when things didn't go her way? And why did he even care?

Dumping a lid on the list of questions forming in his mind, he quickly dialled the number and introduced himself when the King answered on the first ring. 'Your Majesty, this is James Wolfe, head of Wolfe Inc. I have your daughter here. Yes, Gilles is with her. Ava?'

She took the phone with a shaky hand. 'Sir—'

Her voice trembled and despite trying to keep himself detached the sound of it cut Wolfe to the quick.

'Of course. *Oui*. I can get a flight. Yes. Okay.' She rang off and frowned at the phone as if she didn't know what it was doing there.

'Ava?'

She glanced at Gilles as if she didn't know what he was doing there either.

Shock. She was going into shock. Wolfe recognised the signs.

'I have to…' She gave a tiny shake of her head, collected herself. 'I… Frédéric has died. He… I have to organise a flight home.'

Gilles barely blinked, but Wolfe could see his friend's utter devastation below the façade of calm. 'Wolfe, can we borrow your plane?'

'Of course. But there's no we, Gilles. I'll take her.'

'Frédéric was a good friend. I'll—'

'You should be with Anne—'

'I can organise myself,' Ava cut in.

Wolfe's hands clenched into fists when Gilles put his arm around her shoulders. 'Don't be silly, Ava. You can't be alone at a time like this.'

'Shouldn't your priority be to your new wife and your house guests?' Wolfe hated himself for reminding Gilles so flatly. Hated himself for the stab of jealousy over a woman he'd never planned to see again.

'Would you two stop?' Ava demanded. 'I am more than capable of—'

'Getting on my plane and letting me escort you home,' Wolfe commanded.

She scowled up at him. 'I don't want to put you out.'

Wolfe didn't know if she was being stoic or just obstinate, but he knew he wasn't letting Gilles take her to Anders. 'Too late,' he growled.

When the butler approached Gilles again Wolfe stepped closer to Ava, invading her personal space. 'Is that your only suitcase?'

She stepped back. 'I told you before. I don't get off on barbaric men.'

Her view of him grated but he pushed his feelings aside. 'Do you really have time to argue?'

'No.' His words seemed to trigger something inside her and her eyes grew distant. She paced. Looked at Gilles and then turned back to him. 'Fine. You may take me.'

Wolfe mentally shook his head, almost awed at the way she'd managed to turn her acceptance into an order.

Ava was functioning on autopilot and barely registered Wolfe buckling her seat belt while the plane taxied down the runway. Somehow he had got her to Lille and on board a plane without her conscious awareness of it.

Her brother was dead.

The news was shocking. Indescribable.

A helicopter accident. Ava couldn't think about it, her mind incoherent with grief. Her brother was the rock of the family. The future heir. He was five years younger than her and, while they had struggled to be close after her mother died, she had always looked out for him. Anticipated that he would always be there. He couldn't be gone. He was only twenty-four.

She shivered and felt a soft blanket settle over her shoulders. She clutched it.

Wolfe placed a glass of water on the table in front of her. 'Do you need anything else?'

She shook her head. 'I'm fine.'

'So you keep saying.'

But he didn't push it, and Ava was grateful. She watched him return to his seat. When he'd come across her in the foyer her heart had turned giddy at the sight of him. It had taken a lot of effort to remind herself that there was no point in seeing him again and even less in sleeping with him! His increasing anger at her response had thrown her a little but then he'd confirmed that, no, he didn't want more than sex from her, and she'd known she had made the right decision.

After they arrived in Anders she would likely never see him again, and that fact made her feel instantly bereft.

Her mind linked the feeling with a time when she was fourteen and her father had continued with a state trip even though she'd been hospitalised with chicken pox. He'd monitored her condition from afar, as usual, but coming so soon after her mother's death his behaviour had done little to alleviate her loneliness and her sense of powerlessness at being alone.

That same sense of helplessness and loneliness engulfed her now, and she pushed it back. Her father would expect her to demonstrate more fortitude than that.

More childhood memories tumbled into her mind, like dice on a two-up table. Memories of Frédéric as a boy. Of her mother.

Rather than becoming *more* available after her mother's death from cervical cancer, Ava's father had withdrawn and focused on his work, seeming not to know how to connect with her. He had been fine with Frédéric. Ava had grown more and more resentful of the disparity in the way in which he treated his children, and more and more determined to show him that his views of women were archaic and demeaning.

But nothing she did ever seemed to be good enough for him. Perhaps if she'd been more like her mother, had been able to put his needs first, they might have seen eye to eye. But Ava couldn't. She had witnessed her mother's sadness whenever her father chose duty over family, and it had made her want something entirely different for herself.

Now, with Frédéric gone—a thought that just wouldn't stick in her head—she was next in line to the throne. She could only imagine how her father must be cringing over that, and she felt slightly nauseous at the prospect of having to step into the role.

Wolfe's voice telling her to refasten her seat belt cut across her tumultuous thoughts, and she glanced outside her window and saw the Anders mountain range as they came in to land.

Imposing a rigid shut-down on her fears about being home, she blanked her mind and switched to cool indifference. From the plane doorway she could see her father's royal guard standing alongside a line of official black cars, and she nearly turned and asked Wolfe to restart the engine and fly her some place else. Really, she felt about as strong as a daisy in a hail-storm—and she hadn't even seen her father yet.

Sensing Wolfe directly behind her, Ava had a debilitating urge to turn and rush into his arms, have him tell her that everything would be all right. But that was weak, and Wolfe was the wrong man to lean on in this situation. She wasn't special to him, and he wasn't the type to sit back and go unnoticed. He was used to taking charge, and there was no way she was going to let him sideline her in front of her father. She had been handling things on her own for a long time now, and she could handle this, as well.

Images of last night, of falling asleep in his arms after their wonderful lovemaking, filtered through her mind and made her pause. Then the empty space he'd left in the bed that morning intruded and stiffened her resolve. It would be a mistake to think she could rely on James Wolfe even for a short time.

'Thank you for the use of your plane but I can take it from here.'

'I told you I would take you home and I will.'

His hot toffee eyes glittered down at her dangerously, and his controlled voice told her he was as determined to have his way as she was.

'I am home.'

'Ava—'

'Wolfe. I'm fine. Really.'

'You don't look fine. You look like you're about to break apart.'

Did she? She'd have to work on that between here and the palace. Practising now, she squared her shoulders and stared him down. 'I'm not. I thought I told you already. I am not the sensitive type.'

Wolfe arrogantly slashed his hand in the air to cut her off in a move that was reminiscent of something her father would do. 'It's not open for discussion.'

That was *exactly* what her father would say, and *exactly* the reason she couldn't have Wolfe with her. That and the sudden sense that if she let him Wolfe would hurt her as Colyn never had.

'No. It isn't,' she agreed tightly, hardening herself against the sheer force of his will, the sheer force of her desire for him, which appeared to be even worse now that she had experienced what passion really was.

For a moment neither one of them moved, facing off against each other like two adversaries in a gunfight.

Wolfe's mouth tightened as he made to turn away from her. Then his fist clenched and his eyes, when he brought them back to hers, were seething with frustration. 'You are without a doubt the most infuriatingly stubborn female I have ever met.'

His voice, for all its aggression, was as soft as silk and sent a flash of fire beneath the surface of her skin.

He was without a doubt the most beautiful, the most powerfully dangerous male she had ever met, and she was afraid she would dream about him for ever.

CHAPTER FIVE

'DID MATTHIEU SAY what my father wanted to see me about, Lucy?'

'No, ma'am.' Lucy, her new lady's maid, returned from the wardrobe with two jackets for her to choose from.

Ava shook her head and immediately felt terrible as Lucy's face fell. Two weeks home and she still wasn't used to being waited on hand and foot again. She felt sorry for the young girl whose services she'd barely used.

She glanced at her reflection and smoothed her messy ponytail. She hadn't done her hair properly in days, but her father had requested her presence and she would not let him see her as anything less than perfect.

'You don't like my choices, ma'am?'

'I love your choices.' She gave Lucy what she hoped was an appreciative smile. 'But it's hot. In fact, why don't you take the afternoon off? Go and see your boyfriend.'

The girl bobbed her head deferentially and Ava sighed heavily and headed out.

She hated being home.

Hated the cold stone walls of the palace that felt more like a prison. She had barely seen her father since she'd returned, which wasn't necessarily a bad thing—except she had barely seen anyone other than staff, and it had given her far too much time to dwell on her grief.

Glimpsing bright summer sunshine through the long row of Gothic windows as she moved from one hallway to the next made Ava feel bleak. It just felt wrong. The sky should be grey, not blue.

Her brother was dead. The royal duties she had always shied away from were upon her, and there was no escape.

As her father had said, the people needed hope in these black times and she was it. They looked upon *her* to lift them out of the bleak mood caused by the loss of her brother—and, more than that, Ava now knew that her father was ill. One day, sooner than she had expected, she would be Queen—and the thought was completely overwhelming.

What did she know about running a country? Having all those people depend on her? It was criminal how little she knew, and even though that was mainly due to her father's chauvinistic views that women were trophies, not leaders, it gave her no pleasure that he now had to rely on her to preserve Anders' future as an economically viable entity.

And what of her gallery? It was closed for the whole of August, but she had dithered about what to do with it. Although of course she knew in her heart that she would most likely have to close it. It was devastating to think that the life she had built for herself could be so easily dissolved. As if nothing she had done in Paris mattered.

Steadying her breath, she hid her pangs of dismay and a gnawing sense of foreboding behind a smile as she stepped inside her father's plush outer office and greeted his personal assistant.

'He's waiting, Your Royal Highness.'

'Thank you, Matthieu.'

She tried to relax her face as Matthieu opened an inner door and Ava saw her father, as always, behind his enormous rosewood desk. He looked pale and more drawn than usual, and Ava tried to keep her immediate concern from showing in her voice. 'You wished to see me?'

'Yes, Ava. Take a seat.'

'You're starting to worry me, sir,' she said, sitting in one of the leather-bound chairs opposite, wondering why he had greeted her in English. 'Have you received bad news from your physician?'

'No.' Her father's response was clipped. 'I've received disturbing news from the security expert who brought you home from France.'

Wolfe?

Ava's heart leapt behind her rib cage as an image of him that seemed all too close to the surface of her mind clouded her vision. For two weeks he had filled her thoughts right before sleep took her, and he was the first thing she thought of when she woke up. Even on the morning of Frédéric's funeral, when she had felt at her lowest.

Ava sighed. She really needed to stop thinking about those hours they'd spent in bed together. Her dreams of him left her feeling weak and needy, and the man probably couldn't even remember her name, let alone conjure up her image in his head.

Unlike her good self, who could not only conjure up his image oh, so easily, but his scent as well—woodsy and masculine. It was so vivid that he might as well have been in the room with her right now.

'What does Wolfe have to do with anything?'

She had tried to keep the query light, but a sudden fear that her father knew that she had slept with him came at her from left field. Surely Wolfe hadn't told anyone? The tabloids? Could her father's health withstand a salacious story about her at this time?

'I have to do with a lot of things, Your Royal Highness.'

The deep, familiar drawl from the man filling her head space had her twisting around in her seat to where he stood across the room, his body half turned away, as if he'd been doing nothing more than studying the scenery outside the high arched windows.

'But in this case it's about your safety.'

Her eyes drank in his beautifully cut black trousers and white dress shirt that pulled tight across his wide shoulders. He'd had a haircut, the shorter style drawing even more attention to the roguish quality of his perfect bone structure.

Those remembered toffee eyes were fixed on her face, touching her mouth ever so briefly, and Ava felt singed all the way through.

'What about my safety?' She hated that she sounded as breathless as she felt.

'Monsieur Wolfe has some news concerning your car crash at Gilles's château.'

She heard the underlying censure in her father's tone and guessed that he was angry she hadn't told him about the accident herself, but she had no time to ponder that as Wolfe prowled towards her, his loose-limbed gait impossibly graceful for a man his size.

He effortlessly dominated the large room and as he drew closer she realised that her heart was racing. He, of course, could have been a mummy for all the emotion he displayed.

Using years of practice to keep her expression from revealing any of her inner turmoil at having this man—her one-night lover—in the same room as her father, Ava forced herself to maintain eye contact with him. 'Such as?'

'Yesterday I spoke to the mechanic who repaired your car,' he informed her, a touch of fierceness lining his words.

'Why would you do that?'

'A hunch.'

'A hunch?'

'Yes. One that paid off. You didn't crash because of a loss of concentration. You crashed because a vial of potassium permanganate mixed with glycerine had been dropped into your brake master cylinder.'

Ava's brow furrowed. 'Is there a layperson's version of that?'

'Your brakes were tampered with.'

Did he mean deliberately? 'Maybe they were worn.'

'Yes. With a special chemical compound that, when it got hot enough, rendered your brakes useless.'

Ava struggled to digest what he was saying. 'You think my car was deliberately sabotaged?' The very idea was ludicrous. It was true that Anders had once experienced conflict with the neighbouring country of Triole, but that had died down years ago. Her brother had even been set to marry the young Princess of Triole when she came of age.

'Not only that,' her father interjected. 'We now know that Frédéric's helicopter crash was not an accident either.'

'What?' Ava's startled gaze flew to her father. 'I... How is that possible?'

Wolfe's voice was hard when he answered. 'A section of the rotor was altered in such a way that the pilot had no chance of detecting it.'

'You're suggesting Freddie was *murdered*?'

'Not suggesting. Stating. And whoever did it went after you, too.'

Ava reflexively pressed her hand into her stomach. This was too much to take in. 'But that is absurd. Who would do such a thing?'

'Enemies. Freaks. Stalkers. Shall I go on?' His tone was deadly serious.

'Monsieur Wolfe has kindly agreed to investigate that side of things.'

'Wolfe.'

He'd corrected her father. Something no man ever did. Half expecting him to put Wolfe in his place, she was surprised when her father nodded.

Men!

'Really? You volunteered?' Ava didn't bother hiding her incredulity. 'Why would you do that?'

'Ava!' Her father's reprimand at her outspokenness was loud and clear in the still room. 'Wolfe hasn't volunteered. I have hired him.'

Of course. She thought asininely. *Why would a man who keeps his affairs short and shallow volunteer to help out a woman he is clearly finished with?*

It galled her to recall just how many times she had checked her mobile phone for a missed message from him over the past weeks. She could have called him, she supposed, but pride had stopped her from even considering it. Calling him would only prove that she hadn't been able to move on from their night together while he had.

'Why would you do that, sir?' Ava turned her back on Wolfe to try to block out the overwhelming physical attraction she still felt for him. 'Why not use the local police?'

'It's a question of trust, Your Highness,' Wolfe answered.

His frigid formality made her feel despondent, and that in turn made her feel annoyed. 'We don't trust our own police force now? We're a peaceful nation, *Monsieur* Wolfe,' she said, stamping her own formality on the situation. 'No political uprisings anywhere.'

'True. But in this situation you don't know who is intending to hurt you. I won't.'

His tone was bold and confident and she wished she shared his assurance. After the way she had dreamt about him for two weeks she wasn't so sure. Although she did believe he wouldn't hurt her in the way he was referring to.

His thick lashes acted like a shield against his thoughts and Ava couldn't wait for the meeting to end. 'I'm not sure I believe this.' She appealed to her father. 'It could just be coincidence.'

'Chemical compounds kind of mitigate that possibility, Your Highness.' Again Wolfe answered for her father.

'I trust Wolfe's judgement on this, Ava.'

Over her own? What a surprise.

'Fine.' She waved her hand dismissively. 'Is that all, sir?' She needed to get out. Back to the sanctuary of her suite. Wolfe's steely indifference was like a red rag to her overly sensitised senses.

On the one hand she was glad he was treating her like a stranger, but it made her feel inadequate when all *she* could do was remember the feel of his body when it had been joined to hers, his hands on her skin, his mouth... Oh, his mouth!

And Frédéric had been *killed*. Someone might be trying to kill her as well...

'No, that is not all.' Her father brought her attention back to him. 'Wolfe has also been hired as your personal body-guard for the duration of the investigation.'

The breath stalled in her lungs and the room spun. 'I don't think I heard you correctly, sir.'

Neither did Wolfe.

Her *personal* bodyguard?

He glanced at Ava's shocked expression and hoped his own didn't mirror it. The King had requested that he organise personal security for her, not that he be responsible for her himself. He didn't have time for that kind of grunt work on top of his corporate responsibilities. And guarding a woman who already occupied too much of his head space was not something he'd let any of his staff do.

'I know you don't like security being assigned to you Ava,' the King said. 'But things have changed. You are now the Crown Princess and you need to be protected at all times. This situation highlights how important that is.'

'Yes, but we have our own security detail.'

Her father sighed, as if he was settling in for a familiar battle. 'I believe hiring an outsider is the best course of action until this situation is resolved. Wolfe comes highly recommended and is a personal friend of Gilles.'

'I disagree.'

Determination vibrated through her voice and got Wolfe's back up.

The skin on the back of his neck prickled and he resisted the urge to rub it; he was a master at not giving in to those physical signs that demonstrated when a man was under extreme stress. He had tried to convince himself that his sleepless nights with Ava on his mind were just because he had a niggle about her accident. He'd assumed that once that niggle had been investigated and the King was apprised of the danger surrounding his daughter he'd be able to re-establish his normal routine.

The driving need that had hit him in the gut as soon as Ava had stepped into the room made a mockery of that. It wasn't ruminations over her accident that had kept him awake—and hard—for the past two weeks. It was her.

Absently Wolfe wondered if she had relived their night together as much as he had, and whether she'd be interested in taking up where they had left off.

What?

He silently mocked his wishful thinking. By the look of her she'd prefer to run him through with one of those swords lining the King's private study.

Maybe he just needed to get laid.

And, no, not with her. If he took her on as a client—

'Wolfe is clearly too busy, sir. But I'm sure there's another person out there just as capable.'

She was right about him being too busy, Wolfe thought, but there really was no one else he would trust with her life.

Feeling that he no longer had a choice, he gave the King a curt nod of acceptance.

'No!'

The King cut an irritated look at his daughter. 'Ava, this

is not open for discussion. My word is law, and it's time you realised that you have a responsibility, a *duty*, to your country. You *will* do it.'

Did that mean she didn't want to? Wolfe wouldn't have been surprised. He understood the fickle nature of women better than most.

She stood beside the window with her arms crossed and the afternoon sun turning her hair a deep glossy brown. Wolfe could feel her frustration, her fury, in every tautly held muscle of her slender body.

His own body flushed with heat as he took her in, and he couldn't help resenting the effect she had on him. He didn't want to be this caught up by the sight of a woman. *Ever.*

'I'll need absolute control,' he said, overlaying unwanted thoughts with the professionalism he prided himself on. 'Access to everything.' Wolfe addressed his words to the King. 'Every nook and cranny and secret entrance and exit to the castle. Ava's diary. Her itinerary. I'll employ my own chef to do her meals, and I want the final word on everything she does and every person she sees.'

'You're asking a lot.'

Wolfe knew what the King was saying. *This is my daughter and you'd better not stuff up.* 'Yes, I am.'

'Perhaps Monsieur Wolfe would like my firstborn, as well?' Ava said, injecting her voice with bored insolence, tapping her foot agitatedly on the marble floor.

The King nodded his agreement before addressing his mutinous daughter. 'I have organised a ball in your brother's honour this coming weekend and you will need security for that.'

'It's too soon,' Ava whispered softly.

Her arms enfolded her waist in a protective gesture her father didn't seem to notice, but it tugged at some unwanted place inside Wolfe's chest.

'It's not too soon. And the ball is not only to honour your brother's life—it is to find you a husband.'

A *husband*?

Wolfe's eyes locked on Ava's face, which had suddenly turned ashen. His own gut felt as if it was twisted up with his intestines, and a flash of adrenaline rushed through his system as if he'd just been physically assaulted.

'I can find my own husband, sir.'

'Not now that you're Crown Princess, you can't,' the King rasped. 'The stakes have been raised, Ava, and you've had more than enough time to find a suitable partner and Anders badly needs a celebration *and* an heir.'

The tension in the room as Ava stared at her father could have cracked the Arctic shelf. Wolfe thought of the island paradise he had planned to visit next week, after his round of meetings. The warm sparkling blue waters of the North Atlantic. A new set of sun loungers that edged one end of his lap pool.

'Do I even need to be in attendance, sir?' Ava stared down her nose at her father with bored enquiry. 'I'd hate to mess around with your plans.'

The King's eyes hardened. 'Don't be smart, Ava. You have a duty to do. You know that.'

'And is it *my* fault that I am entirely underprepared to carry out that duty?' she retorted.

Her words were underscored by a subtle vulnerability that called to every one of Wolfe's protective instincts and threatened his determination to remain detached from everything at all times. It was an aspect of his nature that had never been challenged before—regardless of what he had seen and experienced. It was the reason he had acquired his nickname.

Instead of following that troublesome thought down what could only be a dead-end street set with an ambush, he focused on what he could see and hear. The facts.

'You chose to run around Paris for eight years.' The King's face had the motley hue of a man on the edge.

'Because I didn't have any choices *here*,' Ava returned icily.

'I won't argue with you, Ava. You need a husband. Someone who understands the business and can support you when you need it.'

Wolfe noticed the King's hand shook slightly as he picked up his water glass. 'Wolfe, if you would accompany my daughter back to her quarters? I'm sure you'll want to get started on the best way to carry out your duties as soon as possible.'

Wolfe wasn't sure about anything right now except two things. His need for this woman was stronger than it had ever been, and taking on the role of her personal bodyguard was absolute insanity.

Ava rounded on him as soon as he'd followed her into her private sitting room. *'"I'll need absolute control. Access to everything."'* She mimicked his voice, her tone scathing. 'Are you kidding me?'

Wolfe couldn't stop himself from running his eyes over her slender curves as she stopped in the middle of the room, her body vibrating with tension.

Had she lost weight?

He studied her face. Her cheeks were flushed, her mouth was tight and she had dark smudges under her eyes that told him she had been sleeping as poorly as he had. All the same, she looked magnificent, and he wanted to take her in his arms and kiss her so soundly it was all he could do to remain where he stood. 'It's for your own good.'

'According to some so is whale oil, but you won't find me firing a harpoon any time soon.'

Wolfe sighed, realising this meeting was going to be even more difficult than he had anticipated. 'Ava, this doesn't have to be awkward.'

She paced away from him and then turned back sharply.

'Don't mistake my fury for awkwardness, Wolfe. I can't believe you've agreed to take this job.' She paused and locked her eyes on his. 'You know, if you wanted to see me again you could have just picked up the phone.' Her navy eyes glittered challengingly.

'My taking this job has nothing to do with whether I want to see you again. And I believe it was you who cancelled dinner,' he reminded her stiffly.

She gave a dismissive shrug. 'I didn't see the point in going out with you when it was a spur-of-the-moment request made out of guilt.'

Wolfe contemplated her answer. Was that why she'd cancelled? 'It wasn't guilt.'

She arched a brow. 'No? So why run off so early? I don't even think the birds were up when you left.'

Wolfe's mouth tightened at the insouciant boredom he heard in her voice. It was the same tone she'd used with her father before. 'I left because I had to provide last-minute details to two of my men before they left on another job.' And he'd wanted to surprise her by replacing her damaged phone with one of his.

Her eyes flicked to his briefly, as if she hadn't considered that. But why would she? In hindsight, it had probably looked bad to her, waking up alone after the passionate night they had spent together. Which, he acknowledged to himself now, was another reason he'd left. He'd woken up with such a strong sense of wellbeing his instinct had been to pull back. It was so ingrained in him he hadn't even thought to question it at the time. Hadn't *wanted* to question it. Now, looking at it from her point of view, her reactions that morning made more sense.

'I'm sorry if I hurt you,' he murmured sincerely.

Ava's chin came up and her eyes shot sparks at him. 'Hurt me? You didn't *hurt* me, Wolfe.'

Wolfe's mouth tightened at her vehemence.

'Quite the contrary. In fact you did me a favour, because I didn't have time to have dinner with you and…' She shrugged again. 'It's too late now anyway.'

Was it?

Yes, of course it was.

'You're right.' For one thing he was now her bodyguard and she was his client, and for another he wanted her just a little too much for comfort. 'That ship has definitely sailed.' Wolfe paced the length of an antique rug, agitated by the situation he had inadvertently created for himself. 'And your father wants you to marry!' Which would effectively remove her from his orbit altogether.

'Something you'll never do!' The heated statement was almost a question.

'Something I'll never do,' he agreed. He'd spent his adult life avoiding that particular institution, and he'd never felt any need to reconsider his views.

Ava nodded sharply, as if somehow his response had been predictable, and Wolfe ground his teeth together. This situation—his total physical awareness of this woman, his total *agitation* at this woman—was going to make his job almost impossible. Never before had he felt as if he was at the mercy of his emotions as he did with Ava, and he hated the feeling that he was not as in control as he would like to think he was. So much for his old nickname. Thank God his army mates couldn't see him now!

Ava started pacing in front of the high bevelled windows again, as if she had too much energy that was searching for an outlet. Her fitted trousers pulled tight across the rounded curves of her backside.

'You do realise if my father knew of our history together there is no way he would let you guard me?'

Wolfe brought his attention back to her face. 'So will you tell him or will I?' he asked silkily, irritated with himself and with her hot-headed stubbornness. She threw him a look and he swiped a hand through his hair. 'Will you just sit down?'

'Another order? Let me just set you straight on something, Monsieur Wolfe.' She set her hands on her sexy hips. 'If you think I am going to do everything you tell me to do you have another thing coming.'

Her accent had thickened with her agitation and it drove his mind right back to the bedroom.

Wolfe released a slow breath. 'Believe it or not, I'm trying to help you.'

'Oh, that's right—my own personal protector.'

He crossed his arms and waited for her to run her anger out, determined not to get into any more arguments with her.

Seeming to sense his newfound resolve, she prodded at it like a child poking its fingers inside a lion's enclosure. 'So, do I get to order you around, as well?'

'I work for your father.'

Her gorgeous mouth thinned. 'Two peas in a pod. How cosy.'

'All that energy you're burning up is just going to tire you out unnecessarily,' he offered amiably.

'You should be glad I'm using it up on pacing,' she snapped.

Wolfe's body caught fire at her words. *Down, boy.* She didn't mean *that* was an alternative. It would probably never be an alternative again after today. No, it definitely *couldn't* be.

He watched her ponytail trail over the soft skin of her neck before he sat on the edge of the low, plump sofa that was surprisingly modern in a room that dated back centuries. 'Take your time. I have all night.'

She crossed her arms over her chest, pushing her breasts up so they swelled just above the opening of her shirt. 'Well, I don't. So I'd like you to leave.'

'I need to ask you a few questions first.'

'You're really pushing your luck.'

'Maybe we should clear the air about that night at Gilles's wedding.'

'Us having sex, you mean?'

Her cool indifference again made him wonder just how many other men she had spent the night with, and the fact that he was at all interested only added another layer of heat to his spiralling annoyance. Was she just like his mother, willing to slake her lust whenever the urge arose and with any man handy? The thought made him sick.

'Yes.'

Her eyebrows rose at his churlish tone and she leant back against the windowsill. 'What's to clear up? Have you forgotten how it's done?'

'Ava—'

'Oh, don't worry, Wolfe. I'm not about to strip off my clothes and ask for a repeat. Unless that's what *you* want? Is that why you took the job?' Her voice dropped, lowering to a sultry purr. 'Are you going to order me to take my clothes off, Monsieur Wolfe?'

'I don't sleep with my clients,' he informed her sternly, ignoring the lie his body's response begged him to make of that statement.

She raised a mocking brow. 'My father will be chuffed to hear that. He's not into men, as far as I know. Although every family has their secrets.'

Her unexpected humour broke the rising tension between them and Wolfe laughed. 'Tell me, Princess, what is it about me being your bodyguard that you hate the most if it isn't our history?'

She threw him a droll look. 'Do you have a spare year?'

Wolfe took a deep breath and offered up an olive branch. 'Why don't we start over?'

'Pretend we've never met?' she asked, somewhat dubiously.

'If that works for you.'

She shrugged. 'As long as you don't order me around I can do that.'

Could she? He wasn't sure he could. 'Good. Take a seat.' He spoke briskly, indicating the sofa opposite him. 'I need to ask you some things to help my investigation.'

When she didn't move Wolfe frowned. Was their cease-fire over so soon?

'Ava?'

'You can call me ma'am. And I believe you just issued another order?'

Yes, perhaps he had.

'So did you,' he ground out.

'You didn't say I couldn't order *you* around.'

'Av— Dammit, you need to cooperate or I can't do my job.' His mind conjured up the last time he'd teased her by telling her that he knew how to make her cooperate and he swallowed. Hard.

'So quit.'

'No.'

'Why not?'

'I've given my word to your father and there's no one else I'd trust with your safety.'

'What do you care about my safety? We're strangers.'

Wolfe sucked in a silent breath. Seriously, the woman would try the patience of a saint. Reminding himself to keep control, he settled back more comfortably on the sofa. The cat sleeping in the corner rose and stretched, sniffed him and then crawled onto his lap.

'Hey, mate.' He stroked it absently. 'You look like you've seen better days.'

'He belonged to my mother.' Her mouth turned down slightly at the corners, indicating that she was still affected by the loss. In some way he envied the fact that she cared.

The cat nudged his hand. 'I take back what I said,' he told the cat. 'You're in top condition for a man your age.'

He looked up to find Ava watching him. When their gazes collided she flushed, and he wondered what she had been thinking.

'I think I hate you.'

Well, that was definitive, and unfortunately the feeling wasn't mutual. 'I'm not your enemy, Ava,' he said softly.

The words *but someone is* lay unspoken between them.

Her shoulders slumped as if she had the weight of the world bearing down on her. 'Can't my father answer your questions?'

'That depends on whether he knows anything about your love-life. From what I saw of the interaction between you two before I would have said you're not that close.'

Her eyes narrowed suspiciously. 'Why do you want to know about my love-life?'

'Everyone in your sphere will be investigated.'

'Even you?'

'I have an alibi for the night Frédéric was killed.'

'Really?' She finally sat down and crossed her legs. Slowly. 'What is it?'

Wolfe regarded her wryly. 'And I don't have any motive for wanting to kill you.'

Yet.

She smiled, clearly sensing his frustration. 'Am I getting to you?'

'You don't want to get to me, Princess.'

'No, I want you to quit.'

'Get over it.'

Suddenly her gaze turned serious. 'Are you planning to investigate my artists?'

'Of course.'

'Be nice. Some of them are sensitive.'

'Unlike you?' It was both a statement and a question.

'Unlike me.'

He didn't believe her. Just the fact that she cared about her artists told him more than anything else. And then there was the look of concern that had briefly crossed her face when she'd first walked into the King's office. She had a heart. She just guarded it well. He could relate to that. He'd put his in a box years ago, and that was exactly where he intended it to stay. It was a timely reminder to keep his head on straight around this woman. She got to him as no one else ever had, and that made her dangerous and him volatile.

'Who was your last lover?'

She threw him a look.

'Before that,' Wolfe said gruffly.

Her eyes widened. 'You want a list?'

No, he did *not* want a damned list. 'Yes.'

She looked as if she was about to tell him to take a hike. 'A lovely American took my virginity when I was eighteen because he thought it would be fun to bed a European princess. Then I met a novelist who wanted to write the great Parisian novel. We were quite serious—unbeknown to my father—but three years ago I realised that we weren't after the same thing and we broke up.'

Wolfe could tell that both men had hurt her and he wanted to run them through with a blunt instrument.

'Did you love him?' The question was irrelevant and he hoped she wouldn't pick up on that.

'How is that relevant?'

Damn. 'If you're going to question me at every turn this won't work.'

'I already know it won't.'

'Ava…'

She huffed out a breath. 'I thought I did at the time. Now… I'm not so sure.'

He wanted to ask what had happened since to make her question that but he wasn't sure he really wanted to know. 'And since then?'

The look she gave him made his stomach knot.

'Apart from the Anders football team...' She recrossed those long legs in the other direction and stared straight at him. 'You're the lucky last, Monsieur Wolfe.'

Wolfe sucked in a litre of air at her admission, ignoring her snipe about the football team. How had he so completely misread her? But he'd known, hadn't he? He'd needed to believe she was as sophisticated and jaded in the art of seduction as he was. It had made it easier to let her go after the night they'd spent together. Made it easier to believe that what was between them was nothing more than mutual biological gratification. Not that it had worked exactly...

He stood up and startled the cat, who promptly jumped down and crossed to Ava. She reached down, her movements as graceful as the animal she scooped into her arms to cuddle.

'I'll need to see your itinerary for the next few days,' he said gruffly.

She didn't look up. 'I'll have Lucy forward it to you tomorrow morning.'

Wolfe moved to the picture window and stared out at the acres of grass that ringed the palace to the sprawling mountains beyond. Incredibly, he was thinking how happy he was that she'd never slept with Gilles.

Hell.

If he was going to protect her he had to stay on task. He had to stop thinking of her as a person. As a desirable woman. And he especially had to stop thinking of her marrying some stupid fool her father was planning to choose for her.

CHAPTER SIX

AVA WASN'T SURE how she was supposed to find a husband when she compared every man she came across to Wolfe. Not that she had taken her father's oppressive statement seriously. She had no intention of letting herself be bullied into a convenient marriage just to suit his wishes. Not on something this important.

Fortunately she was getting a reprieve from having to pretend to go along with it in the arms of her debonair cousin Baden.

'Quite the *soirée* your papa has put on for you, cuz.'

'Yes,' Ava agreed flatly, glancing around the gilt-edged ballroom filled to the gills with beautifully attired guests. Alcohol consumption had lifted the mood considerably since the beginning of the night, and even though she hated being here she had to admire her father's opportunistic streak.

He was a man who didn't stop until he got what he wanted. And he wanted her married, it seemed. In a hurry. Of course the supreme and lately suppressed romantic in her knew that there was every possibility she would meet someone tonight and fall in love at first sight. After all it had happened to Anne and Gilles. But… Her eyes drifted to Wolfe, standing nonchalantly towards the back of the room.

There was her problem, right there.

He was supposed to look like one of the guests. Under-cover. What he looked like was a man who could kill with his bare hands and not put a crease in his bespoke tuxedo. But perhaps that was only because she knew it was true. Perhaps to the other women watching him so closely he just looked like a sexy, rakish male who was good in bed. Something else she knew to be true…

As if sensing her appraisal, he meshed his eyes with hers. Ava felt the impact of his stare from across the room. She couldn't fathom the effect he still had on her. It was instantaneous and totally consuming. She sensed that he felt it, too, but he had much more control over it than she did. Or the attraction just wasn't as strong for him as it was for her. Given that he was only here because her father was paying him, she put more weight on the latter.

And at night dreamt of shedding him of the former…

'Who is he?'

'Who?' Ava gripped Baden's hand and swung him so that Baden had his back to Wolfe.

'The cowboy leaning against the wall who hasn't taken his eyes off you all night.'

Ava glanced over Baden's shoulder as if she was searching for whoever he was talking about. 'I don't see anyone special, but then Father has every single man on the planet in attendance tonight. How are you enjoying the evening?'

Baden scoffed. 'It's a little soon after Freddie's death, but… You're trying to change the subject, dear cousin. There's a story here you don't want me to know about. Come on.' He tickled her ribs as he'd used to do when they were children. 'Tell Cousin Baden.'

'*Arrête*, Baden. This is hardly the place.' Ava hadn't meant to snap, but Baden wasn't the most socially savvy individual at the best of times. 'You're letting that wild imagination of yours run away with you again.'

'I don't like him.'

'I don't either,' she grumbled, knowing that it wasn't dislike she felt for James Wolfe, but something else entirely.

If only he wasn't so arrogant. So self-assured. So lethally male. Ava sighed. Who was she trying to kid? She loved those aspects of Wolfe's nature. Colyn had never been so overcome with passion that he had dragged her from a dance floor and kissed her senseless the way Wolfe had.

'You slept with him, didn't you?' Baden mused. 'I can see it in your eyes.'

Pressing her fingers to her forehead, Ava wondered if it was possible for a headache to materialise out of thin air. 'Please, Baden…' There was no way she was going to confirm anything to her blabber-mouth cousin. 'Keep your voice down.'

'You don't want your papa to find out?'

'He's…' Ava struggled to come up with some plausible reason as to why Baden might see Wolfe around the palace over the next little while without informing him as to why he was really here. 'He's trying out for a staffing position, I believe.'

'You slept with the hired help. You naughty girl.' Baden laughed. 'Not that I can't see the attraction. All that hard muscle!'

Ava cringed as she realised that Wolfe had moved to within hearing distance. 'Would you *please* keep your voice down?' she pleaded.

'What position is he going for?'

'I don't know and I don't care. Ask Father.' Ava knew that he wouldn't, because he had never had an easy relationship with her father.

Baden sipped his wine. 'How is the old tyrant bearing up?'

Relieved to be talking about anything other than Wolfe, Ava latched on to the change in topic. 'You never know with

Father. But honestly I think he's in denial. Hence the party tonight.' She swept the lavish ballroom with a rueful glance.

'And you? How do you feel about being Anders' first Queen?'

Baden knew her life at the palace had never been easy. It had always been something that had bonded them together since he had lost his own father, her father's twin brother, when he was five. Then his mother had deserted him, taking his baby sister with her, and he hadn't seen either of them since.

'Oh, I'm definitely in denial.' She gave a dismissive shrug, not wanting to dwell on the future when she still had no answers about how to handle it. 'Can you excuse me? I need the powder room. Why don't you ask the lovely Countess over there to dance?'

Baden followed her gaze and raised an eyebrow. 'Because she's ugly.'

'Baden!' Ava rebuked him again. 'That's a terrible thing to say.'

'If you don't like the truth, don't get in the way of it.'

Ava gave him a look that told him exactly what she thought of his tasteless comment, and then kept her gaze down as she wound her way purposefully through the throng of guests. She didn't have a specific destination in mind but somewhere quiet and—

'I told you not to go outside.'

The sound of Wolfe's deep voice directly behind her shimmered down her spine.

Ava looked up and realised she had been so preoccupied with Baden's horrible comment that she had walked outside the glass doors leading to her mother's rose garden. A golden moon hung like an enormous balloon on the horizon, and fairy lights twinkled strategically from various trees and bushes, giving the summer evening an ambient glow.

'I needed some air.'

'Is it any wonder?'

She stopped walking and looked back at him. 'What does that mean?'

'It means I'm surprised you're still standing after all the dancing you've done. Husband-hunting looks like difficult work.'

Ava glared at him. Really, she wasn't in the mood for the uncivilised version of Wolfe tonight. 'Why are you even here still?' she asked, her English skewed by her testiness. 'I thought you were the best, but so far you haven't come up with anything, and it has been a week already.'

A long week, in which she had once again locked herself in her room in a petulant sulk. Partly she still wasn't ready to embrace the duties her father wanted her to take on, and partly she had been hoping that Wolfe would get so bored he would quit.

'Unfortunately the invitation I put out over the internet for the bastards responsible to come forward hasn't seemed to work. Maybe I'm losing my touch.'

'Maybe you never had it.' As soon as the words were out she regretted her provocative tone because his golden eyes sparkled with amusement. 'Now, that's just plain nasty, Princess. Fortunately my ego is strong enough to withstand that kind of a slur.'

She snorted. 'Your ego is like a cockroach. It could withstand a nuclear holocaust.'

Completely unprepared for Wolfe to throw his head back and laugh, Ava struggled to prevent a smile from forming on her lips. 'Stop that.' She absolutely loved his deep chuckle. 'People are looking.'

Not waiting for him to follow her instructions, she continued down the stone steps past small clusters of guests enjoying the fragrant garden.

'So, any contenders you need me to vet for you?'

Wolfe's lazy drawl sounded too close, and Ava stopped and swung around to face him.

It took a minute for her to ascertain his meaning and when she did she gasped. '*You're* vetting my future husband?'

'It's part of the package.'

Ava bit back the first retort that came to mind, knowing it wouldn't lead anywhere good. 'Well, it's a useless part,' she informed him shortly. 'Just because my father says something should happen it doesn't mean that it will.'

'You're against marriage?' His brow rose in surprise.

'No, I'm against marriage without love.'

'Ah, a romantic. I somehow didn't take you for that.'

'You don't know me very well, that's why,' she said stiffly.

The look he gave her told her that he knew part of her very well, and was remembering it just as vividly as she was.

Ava felt a blush creep up her neck and quickly added, 'And you don't have to be romantic to want to fall in love.'

'No, just deluded.'

The wealth of emotion behind his brief response made her hesitate. Everyone had a story that coloured their actions and decisions, and she had a sudden urge to know what his was. 'Is it that you're afraid of intimacy, or that you like variety too much to settle down?'

'Since I'm not afraid of anything, and I move around continuously, I think it's safe to go with the latter.'

Ava studied his brooding expression and knew he was afraid of one thing at least—revealing anything personal about himself.

'Choosing that kind of lifestyle would indicate that you're running away from something.' She watched his response to her comment and just saw bland enquiry. Then another idea popped into her head. 'Or is it more that you're searching for something to add meaning to your life?'

The slight narrowing of his eyes was the only sign that she might have punctured his cool reserve in some form.

'Why complicate things unnecessarily, Princess? It's always better to lead with the head, not the heart.'

His use of the word *Princess* in his sardonic drawl told her it would be pointless to push him. He was a man who did what he wanted regardless of anyone else. 'You should take coffee with my father,' she said with measured indifference. 'You'd get on well.'

His piercing gaze scanned her face and she knew he'd picked up on the bitterness that was never far from the surface at the mention of her father.

'What's up between you and your old man?'

About to tell him that she didn't answer personal questions either, Ava found herself responding anyway. 'The truth is we've never seen eye to eye. He is a man who is very set in his ways. Very practical and logical. I was never his idea of the perfect daughter.'

'Why not?'

She could see his curiosity was well stirred and paused. She never talked about her relationship with her father—or lack thereof. Ever. But some small part of her wanted Wolfe to understand her. She'd seen the look on his face when she'd revealed how few lovers she'd had in her twenty-nine years— as if he'd expected there to have been a cast of thousands— and she hated that she cared what he thought of her. But it was senseless to deny that she didn't—at least to herself.

'I was too much of a tomboy growing up. Too impetuous. I liked bareback horse-riding and climbing trees and he wanted me to dress in pretty clothes and speak only when spoken to. I did like the pretty clothes, but...' Her voice trailed off.

Wolfe gave her a small smile. 'The speaking when spoken to...?'

She returned his smile, but it felt hollow. The pain of the past still had too tight a grip for her to find any lightness in those memories. 'Not so much. When my mother died he got worse. My brother was sent to a military academy to start his leadership training and I was home-schooled because my job was to look pretty, not to go out and work. Nothing I ever did was good enough in his eyes. Do you know he's never once visited my gallery in Paris—?' She cut herself off with a self-conscious laugh when she realised just how much she had revealed to him. Why not blurt out that she was afraid she'd never find love either, and tell him *all* her deepest fears?

'Does that make you feel like you're still a disappointment to him now?'

Ava felt her stomach churn. 'No. I don't need his praise. I'm not a child.' She cleared the strident note out of her voice. 'But I resent that he wants everything his way.' She bent and sniffed at one of her mother's prized flowers, the scent faint now in the late evening. 'Why do you think he wants me to marry?'

'To make sure the monarchy is secure.'

'To make sure there is someone beside me who can do the job, you mean.'

'You think he doesn't believe you're capable?' Wolfe's brows rose in surprise.

'I'm a woman. That speaks for itself as far as my father is concerned.'

Wolfe seemed to consider this and Ava moved farther along the path, wishing she'd never let this conversation progress as far as it had.

'Do you?'

His question stopped her and she glanced back at him. 'Do I what?'

'Think you're capable?'

'Yes,' she said, internally cringing at the defensiveness in her tone. She had a Fine Arts degree and a Master's in Business and while she might not know everything involved in running a country, she... 'I run a successful gallery.' Which surely counted for something.

'A small business,' he dismissed, shoving his hands in his pockets and strolling closer. 'It hardly translates, wouldn't you say?'

A wave of heat coursed through Ava at the slight. She might struggle to feel worthy in her personal relationships, but hadn't she always backed herself professionally. 'No, I would not say that.' She didn't even try to keep the indignation out of her voice. 'Do you know how hard I had to work to prove myself in Paris? To make my *"small"* business successful?' She straightened her spine. 'How difficult it was to get anyone to take me seriously? To get artists to trust me to work for them when everyone just expected me to be a vacuous party girl?'

She was breathing so hard when she'd finished she nearly missed Wolfe's soft grin.

'Oh, you are *horrible*!' she spluttered. 'You were playing devil's advocate with me!'

'You have a fire in your belly I guess you would never show your father.'

It pained her to acknowledge he was right. She had built a wall up where her father was concerned and she used it to keep him out. To show him that she didn't need him. More than that, she was afraid he would shoot her down in flames if she tried and failed in replacing Frédéric.

She was a grown woman who had never got over wanting her father's approval. She'd moved to Paris so she could avoid facing that.

Feeling dismayed by her unexpected realisations she shook her head. 'He doesn't respect me.' And, boy, did that hurt.

'So make him.'

Ava's startled gaze connected with Wolfe's.

'And if you stop pretending you're not sensitive about things when you are, that might help.'

She felt her mouth fall open at his gentle ribbing and quickly snapped it closed. She wanted to argue that she'd mastered that unwelcome aspect of her nature years ago, but just looking at Wolfe made her awash with a certain type of sensitivity she couldn't deny.

She turned away, only to have him grasp her shoulders and turn her back before she'd taken a single step. He reached out and secured her chin lightly between his fingers, his eyes glittering down at her in the glow of the mood lighting. 'Maybe you need to think of your duty as being to your people now, Ava, not your father.'

Her breath caught. He hadn't called her Ava since that morning at Gilles's. Trying to hold on to her equilibrium, and reminding herself that there was nothing intimate behind his unexpected tenderness, she gave a rueful quirk of her lips. 'I never looked at it like that.'

'Because you're focusing on the past. That's gone. It's only the future that counts.' His tone was firm, the words delivered with such a resounding sense of resolution she knew he had said them before.

'You're right.' She let the silence build between them as her head spun with ideas. His words *'make him'* settled inside her. Perhaps if she stopped reverting to the recalcitrant teenager she had once been that would be a start. 'I cannot keep fighting my father. It is not only futile, but he's sick. And I do have obligations now that require my full attention.' She released a noisy breath and smiled wearily. 'Do you think perhaps I have felt sorry for myself for long enough?'

Wolfe's head came up, surprise lighting his gaze, as if he hadn't expected her to admit to such a flaw. Then he laughed. 'You're one out of the box, Princess.'

She smiled back at him, warmed by the admiration in his voice. Warmed by the fact that he somehow made her feel valued.

She was instantly transported to the single night they had

shared together. As much as the passion between them had shocked her, it had also thrilled her. She wondered— *No, Ava.* Not only was Wolfe not interested in fostering a long-term relationship with a woman, he had said himself that their *'ship'* had *'definitely sailed'*.

CHAPTER SEVEN

'WE ARE NOT stopping, Ava, and that's that.'

Ava knew her father's face had taken on the stony hue that had used to scare her as a child, but she steadfastly kept smiling at the sea of people waving flags along the tree-lined boulevard as the royal coach trotted slowly down the centre of Anders.

Every year citizens and tourists came out in droves to celebrate Anders Independence Day, with a plethora of sumptuously themed floats and gaily designed costumes. This year there was a more sombre mood to the proceedings, with many of the floats carrying her brother's picture. It made Ava want to reach out to her people to make up for Frédéric's loss. After her conversation with Wolfe three nights ago she knew that she could either let her insecurities control her or...try.

So she had.

And it felt like a blessed release finally to make some of the hard decisions she hadn't realised she'd been actively resisting. One had been to inform her artists that she would be helping them find new representation when her gallery closed down the following month, and the other had been to start sitting in on business meetings with her father's advisors. The workload was intense, and there were aspects of ruling her country that made her head spin, but she felt as if she was making inroads. Slowly.

Slow inroads into everything except her relationship with her father. Just this morning he had been lecturing her about making a decision on the five 'expressions of interest,' as he referred to the marriage proposals he had already received on her behalf, without even considering her view. As far as he was concerned she should bow down to her destiny, and he saw nothing wrong with the fact that one of those proposals had arrived from a man she hadn't even met!

But Ava wasn't ready to compromise on that point. And with Wolfe sitting opposite her, sublime in a designer suit, his gaze scanning back and forth over the joyous crowd, she didn't even want to think about it.

Instead she marshalled her determination to make her father respect her and kept a calm smile on her face as she addressed him. 'I need to walk some of the way.'

Her father nodded benevolently to his people. 'I won't repeat myself, Ava.'

'I know it's not the way we've traditionally done the avenue ride,' she said. 'But if I am going to rule Anders it's important to me that our people don't see me as a distant figure. Especially since I have lived in Paris for so long.'

Her father glanced at Wolfe. 'Tell her it's too dangerous.'

'The King has a point,' Wolfe conceded. 'It is never a good idea to make last-minute changes to your itinerary.'

Ava felt her stomach plunge as he sided with her father, instantly recognising the emotion that gripped her as a feeling of betrayal. After the gala ball she felt as if they had formed a friendship of sorts. She had enjoyed his company as he had escorted her to and from meetings, had enjoyed him sitting in with her to ensure her safety, and been surprised and thankful when on a couple of occasions he'd offered some keen business insights that had been beyond her understanding at the time.

Most of all, though, she loved how when everyone else had left for the day he brought her a cup of her favourite tea without her having to ask. Nobody, she had realised that first time, ever did anything for her without her having to ask first.

She looked across at him, willing him to understand. 'But it *can* be done.'

Her father's face tightened. 'Why are you always so determined to defy me?'

'This is not about defiance, sir,' Ava insisted, holding back her tendency to disconnect from her father in order to keep her goal in sight. 'If you can give me one good reason why I shouldn't walk amongst our people then I'll listen.'

'It's a break in tradition.'

'Why can't I start a new one?'

'A safety risk, then.'

Of course Ava knew he was right, but she also recognised that fear was debilitating. 'Is it important to rule safely, Father?' she asked softly. 'Or with integrity?'

Her father turned from the window and stared at her, his expression pained. 'You always were a smart child, Ava, but you're still not leaving this carriage. Wolfe—' he spoke while still smiling and waving '—stop her before she does something stupid.'

Ava hated the fact that yet another man held something so important to her in his power. She lifted her chin, wondering how she would react when Wolfe sounded the death knell to her idea. It was important to her on so many levels...

Fortunately her determination wasn't to be tested on this as Wolfe, his expression stern, broke her steady gaze to address her father. 'My job is to keep her safe, Your Majesty, not to stop her.'

'Thank you.'

Wolfe turned from the narrow window that had once formed part of a parapet when he heard Ava step into the small room he was using as an office. He'd thought she would want to make an early night of it, worn out after walking for miles that day and thrilling her people with handshakes and good wishes. On the contrary, she looked fresh and still buzzed, dressed in some sort of yoga outfit that left little to his hyperactive imagination.

He knew why she was thanking him, but she'd put him in an impossible position with her earnest request and he was still fuming about it. 'It was a foolish thing to do.'

'Maybe.' She threw him a brief smile. 'But I needed to do it and you understood that.'

'I understood you had a crazy idea and it came off okay this time. Next time it might not.'

'Life's a risk, no?' She cocked her head. 'I would have thought your job was full of them.'

'Calculated risks are different from spontaneous reactions.'

'It wasn't a spontaneous reaction,' she said indignantly. 'I'd thought about it all morning.'

'Next time you might want to share that,' he said dryly.

'Okay.' She shrugged. 'I take your point, but it doesn't stop me from being happy that I did it.'

Wolfe grunted in response and made the mistake of moving to stand behind his desk. He'd had to train himself to ignore her delicious scent all week, but this close, in the confines of this suddenly overheated room, it was nearly impossible to do.

When she didn't make a move to leave he glanced at her. 'Was there something else?'

'Yes. Do you have any news on who might have killed my brother?'

'No.' He had some leads to go on but he had no intention of telling her that. Keeping a client apprised of his intel was not the way he operated.

'Okay, then.'

Her slender fingers trailed over the top of his desk, but just when he thought she was going to give him a break and leave she swung back towards him.

'I'm going for a walk outside. Just in case you need to know.'

Of course he needed to know.

'If you go I'll have to go with you.'

Her eyes met his. 'Okay.'

Her voice had a husky quality, and all he wanted to do was haul her across his desk and push that stretchy top up her chest. 'I suggest you get a jacket. It's cold outside.'

'I don't know where you get your weather information from,' Ava said ten minutes later, her sneaker-shod feet crunching the gravel footpath underfoot. 'It's not cold at all.'

She shrugged out of her lightweight jacket and draped it loosely over her shoulders. 'I love these cloudless summer nights in Anders. The cicadas singing and the mountains in the background. When I was small I used to lie on the grass with my mother and count the stars. It's not possible to do that in Paris.'

'No stars?'

'It's not the stars; it's the grass. If you so much as look the wrong way at the lush lawns in a Parisian park a *gendarme* will come over and slap you with a misdemeanour charge.' She wagged her finger playfully. 'One can look but never touch.'

Wolfe knew exactly how that felt.

'Even princesses?'

She threw him an impish grin. 'Afraid so. The only people who get special treatment in Paris are the Parisians.'

Wolfe laughed, finding himself relaxing under the vast velvet sky, intrigued as Ava relived her time in Paris and made comparisons between France and Anders. He'd found himself making similar comparisons between Australia and Anders during the week. It was most likely because it had been years since he'd spent so long in one place, but as much as he would have said he was a beach lover he found the small mountainous nation of Anders surprisingly serene and peaceful.

'How do you feel about being back?' he asked.

Ava stopped walking and turned to face the mountains, their high peaks barely discernible in the night sky. 'Two weeks ago I would have said I hated it, but now...now it's growing on me again.'

She hesitated, and he could see her wrestling with herself about whether to continue. Surprisingly he wanted her to. He liked listening to her talk.

'Because?'

'Because I've missed the fresh scent of pine in the air and the tranquillity of being surrounded by every shade of green. It feels like home, and being here has made me realise that I miss that more than I allowed myself to think about.' Her hand trailed a clump of lavender and she raised her fingers to her nose and inhaled the sweet scent. 'The only fly in the ointment is my father,' she continued, almost to herself. 'He's so determined that he's always right it becomes exhausting trying to deal with him at times. What about you?' she asked lightly.

'No. I find him easy to get along with,' Wolfe deadpanned.

She stopped in the middle of the path and arched her brow. 'You know what I mean.'

He did. He just had no intention of talking about his parents.

Stepping off the path onto the well-tended lawn, he walked a short distance and laid his palms against the trunk of an ancient pine tree. He wasn't sure if she would follow, but then he heard her soft tread on the pine needles and felt glad that she had. 'They say if you hold your hands against the trunk like this you can feel its secrets.'

'Really?'

She spread her fingers wide against the trunk beside his and stirred up all sorts of unwelcome responses inside his body.

'What do you feel?'

Wolfe paused, quite sure she didn't want to hear what he was really feeling. 'Bark.'

She laughed and shook her head. 'And for a minute there I thought you were going to go all deep and meaningful on me.'

'Mmm, not me.' Wolfe caught her lingering gaze and moved back to the worn path.

'You grew up on a farm, didn't you?'

'Yep.' He hoped his short answer gave away just how little he wanted to talk about his past.

'What was it like?'

No such luck...

'Dusty.'

'Pah!'

He glanced at her and couldn't help chuckling at her disgusted expression.

'Do you know you close up like a crab whenever I ask you anything personal?'

'Clam.'

'That's what I said.' She studied him as if she was trying to work him out. 'Why do you make it so hard to know you?'

Wondering what to say to that thorny question, Wolfe was relieved when his cell phone vibrated in his pocket. He pulled it out and saw that it was his brother. 'Excuse me, but I have to take this.' He pressed the answer button. 'Ad-man, what's up?'

His brother hesitated on the other end of the line. 'Oh, sorry, bro. Have I caught you in the middle of a run?'

It took Wolfe a second to understand his brother's comment, and then he became conscious that his breathing was tense and uneven. *Great.* 'Just work. Don't tell me you're still in the office, too?'

'With you living it large in a European castle, guarding a beautiful maiden, where else would I be?'

Wolfe told his brother he'd trade places with him in the blink of an eye but even as he said it he knew he was lying. Quickly changing the subject, he tormented his brother a little more and then ran through a few work-related issues before ringing off.

'Well, that was convenient.'

Wolfe lifted his gaze to the woman who was slowly driving him mad and realised that other than his brother she was the only person who had ever teased him about his behaviour.

Feeling overly hot, even though the air temperature had dropped a couple of degrees, he focused on the small cluster of flowers she held in her hands, not unlike a bride waiting to walk down the aisle. Shaking off that disconcerting image, he made his voice curt when he spoke. 'We should head back inside.'

'Okay.' She sniffed the small posy and fell into step beside him. 'Was that your brother?'

He thought about changing the subject, but knew if he did her interest would only grow, not wane. 'Yes.'

'You sound close to him.'

'I am.'

'So, no sibling rivalry?'

He shook his head. 'We're less than two years apart so we did everything together.'

'Does he travel around like you?'

'No. He's based in New York.'

'Does he have a wife? Kids?'

Wolf stopped so abruptly she'd taken two more steps before she noticed.

'This is starting to feel like an inquisition.'

She shrugged one slender shoulder. 'I'm just trying to know you a little better.'

'By asking questions about my brother?'

'You won't answer questions about anything else.'

That was because he had never seen the point in talking about himself. And, if he was completely honest, because he was starting to like her in a way that transcended the physical and that scared him. It was dangerous to bond with a client. It caused sloppy work and unrealistic attachments to develop.

'Look, don't worry about it.' She gave him a half smile that seemed paper-thin. 'When you're like this…' She gave another one of those Gallic shrugs that drove him bonkers. 'I forget you work for my father.'

If she had tried to wheedle information from him, or tried to make him feel guilty, he would have held his line. Faced with the stoic indifference he now knew she used to mask her true feelings, he caved. Or perhaps it was just that she looked so beautiful in the light of the crescent moon.

'What do you want to know?' he asked, not a little gruffly.

'What do you want to tell me?'

Wolfe blew out a breath. It was so typical of her to make him work for something he didn't even want.

'My father died ten years ago.'

Ava stopped and looked at him. 'I'm sorry. Were you close?'

Had they been close? Probably not, if he had to think about his answer. 'At times.'

'And your mother?'

Wolfe turned to continue walking. 'I don't know where she lives. She left when I was younger.'

'Oh. That must have been hard.'

'It is what it is.'

He felt her glance and knew she was seeing more than he wanted her to. 'Is she the reason you avoid long-term relationships?'

There was a lengthy silence in which he realised even the cicadas had stopped singing. As if they too were waiting with bated breath for his answer. Wolfe made a sound in his throat at the uncharacteristically fanciful thought and nearly missed her next word.

'Love?'

He did not want to talk about this with her. It was time

to end the conversation. 'Love is the most unstable emotion I've ever come across,' he said fiercely. 'My mother didn't just leave once. She left over and over. And every time she returned she told us how much she loved us. It was the only time she ever said it.'

As soon as the bleak words were out he regretted them. The look of pity on Ava's face only made the feeling ten times worse.

'Where did she go?'

Wolfe thrust his hand through his hair and promised himself next time he'd stick to monosyllabic answers or none at all, as he usually did. 'We never knew. Sometimes she would meet a man in town and take off, other times she just went on a "holiday".'

'But that's awful. What did your father say? Was he even there?'

'He was there,' Wolfe said grimly. *Usually out on his tractor, ignoring reality.* 'But he didn't say anything. When she came back, sometimes months later, we all just pretended she'd never left.'

'That hurts the most, no?' Her delicate brows drew together in consternation. 'I used to hate it when my father would go off on extended business trips, or lock himself away in meetings and then totally ignore how it made us feel.'

'I wasn't hurt by her actions,' Wolfe denied. 'But Adam was. Whenever she'd go he used to run away and try and find her.' He hated remembering those hours of searching for his brother, worried about whether he'd find him alive or dead in the hot, arid bushland that surrounded their farm.

'But not you?'

Wolfe realised with a start that she had somehow sucked him back into the past against his better judgment, and he felt excessively relieved to find they had arrived back at the palace. 'No. Not me. I was older. I understood.'

She looked up at him with such a penetrating gaze he felt every one of his muscles grow taut.

'Understood what, Wolfe?' Her gaze bored into his. 'That you were a child who couldn't rely on his mother's love?'

CHAPTER EIGHT

AVA VACILLATED BETWEEN the two evening gowns laid out on her hotel bed. She could smell the fragrant Parisian air through her open window, and outside she knew the night sky was streaked with pink and orange, the Seine sparkling under the glow of the street lamps that had just gone on.

She tapped her foot in time with her favourite jazz album, blaring from the hotel's sound system, trying to feel okay about her coming dinner with Prince Lorenzo of Triole and not to torture herself about where Wolfe had got to last night.

For a whole week he'd barely uttered a word to her—ever since he'd opened up about his childhood and she'd made that rash statement about his mother. The words had been out of her mouth before she'd thought it through, but she had felt so outraged on his behalf. And clearly he'd felt outraged by what *she'd* said, because he had stopped sitting beside her in meetings and had even stopped making her evening cup of tea. It was a silly, inconsequential thing to care about, but it had come to mean a lot to her. His support had come to mean a lot. Somewhere along the way she had forgotten that she was just his client. Forgotten that, although they had been lovers, they had nothing else between them.

The devil on her shoulder told her he'd been out with a woman. That he was a man with a large sexual appetite he had not slaked for weeks. Her hands knotted into fists and she forced herself not to think about the heaviness in her heart. Forced herself to concentrate on the *crucial* task of choosing a gown for the evening. She smiled wryly at Lucy, who clutched the ornate mahogany bedpost with a dreamy expression on her face.

Ever since Ava had submitted to the changes in her life and accepted Lucy's help their relationship had blossomed into the beginnings of a genuine friendship.

'Which do you think, Lucy?'

'Depends on the look you're going for. The silver is stylish and understated, while the red is very "look at me". Very racy.'

Which would Wolfe prefer? The thought winged into Ava's mind before she could stop it. The silver. He'd want her to blend into the background.

'The red,' she said decisively, angry with herself for wanting to dress to please Wolfe. And *racy* might help pick up her mood. Ava rolled her shoulders to ease the tension her warm bath had failed to alleviate.

'Great choice.' Lucy beamed. 'Prince Lorenzo will find you irresistible!'

The sound of the music being clicked off made Lucy's last words ring loudly in the sudden silence. Lucy gasped, her hand pressed against her chest. 'Monsieur Wolfe!'

'Leave us, Lucy,' Wolfe commanded icily.

Lucy hesitated, her eyes darting to Ava's.

Ava handed Lucy the red gown. 'If you could have this pressed and return it when it's done, Lucy, that would be lovely.'

She could tell instantly that Wolfe was in a dangerous mood; the expression on his face was as black as his clothing.

After waiting for Lucy to close the sitting room door, she turned to face him. 'I didn't hear you knock.'

'That's because I didn't.'

Their eyes connected and Ava couldn't have looked away

to save her life. Then he prowled to the other side of the room and slammed her window closed before turning to face her. 'Big night tonight?' His eyes fell on the silver dress draped over her bed.

'A state dinner is always important.' Her heart thumped in her chest and she moved to sit on the stool facing the dressing table, started unwinding her hair from the topknot she'd put it in while she bathed. If nothing else it gave her hands something to do. Although she knew he was angry, she had no idea why. 'Did you want something?'

Now, *there* was a loaded question. But it wasn't one Wolfe was in a state of mind to answer. Not with her wearing that flimsy midnight-blue kimono that perfectly matched her eyes and most likely nothing underneath.

He was in a foul mood and he knew why. He was frustrated with the lack of progress he'd made on her case—and frustrated with himself. He'd lost focus somewhere in the middle of last week and stopped thinking of her as a job. Somewhere along the way he'd started to admire her work ethic, her commitment to master a duty she'd never thought would be hers…and then he'd gone and exacerbated the situation by spilling his guts to her.

'Understood what, Wolfe? That you were a child who couldn't rely on his mother's love?'

Wolfe silently cursed as her nosy question replayed once again inside his head. That's what you got for opening up to a woman. Psychobabble and a week-long headache.

He'd made a mistake—too many where she was concerned—but as long as he made the other night his last he could live with it.

Now all he had to do was to reinstate the cool professionalism he was renowned for and get back on task.

In some ways he had hoped taking last night off would help with that. He'd met a mate in Rome at a nightclub he'd hated before he'd even made it past the officious bouncer. When he'd hit the dance floor with a super-sexy Italian girl his head had started aching from the loud music and his body had all but yawned with boredom. Boredom? At breasts bursting out of a short dress that would send any normal man into a frenzy of desire? Ridiculous. Or so Tom had informed him.

'Wolfe?'

His name falling from Ava's delectable lips was like a husky invitation to his senses. In his mind's eye he imagined her rising gracefully from the cushioned stool on which she sat. Saw her loosen the sash on her robe, knew that it would fall halfway open, catch on the crest of her nipples and hold, revealing the temptation of her flat belly and the brunette curls he longed to bury his face in. She would hold his gaze, tilt her cute nose and saunter towards him. Then she'd arch her imperious brow, wrap her arms around his neck and pull his mouth to hers.

Of course she didn't do any such thing.

Instead she picked up her hairbrush and ran it through her hair in long, languid strokes. Wolfe glanced sideways and saw the discarded jodhpurs and billowy white shirt she had worn riding earlier that day with suitor number two hundred and one, and all he wanted to do was ride *her*. Hard.

For nearly three weeks he'd held it together. Held his desire for her at bay. Held his self-control in check. Why was it pulling at him now? Making him sweat?

But he knew, didn't he?

Lorenzo, the urbane Prince of Triole, wanted her—and her father had decided he was the one. He'd asked Wolfe to do a special security check on him to clear the way. Tonight Lorenzo would no doubt try to stake his claim on her. Knowing how much she sought her father's approval, how much she wanted to do the right thing by her country, he was very much afraid she'd go along with it. Not that he should care. It wasn't as if he had made a claim on her himself.

'Wolfe?' Her voice had risen with concern at his delayed response to her question. 'Do you have news about who caused Frédéric's accident?'

'No.' Wolfe grated harshly, holding up the crumpled piece of paper he'd printed out five minutes ago. 'I'm here about this.'

She glanced at the document before cutting her eyes back to him. 'Am I supposed to know what *"this"* is?'

'Your itinerary.'

'Oh, that.' She turned back to the mirror dismissively. 'You told me to tell you in advance when I planned to make changes to it.'

'I remember telling you it was dangerous to change it.'

Her nonchalant shrug ratcheted up his tension levels. 'It's going to be a lovely day tomorrow and—'

'You've been to Paris before,' he interrupted impatiently. 'Hell, you lived here for eight years. Why do you need to go on some convoluted walking tour?'

'I have not been here for nearly a month. I want to see the city again.'

Wolfe bit back a string of curses at her determined expression. 'Look out of the window.' He gestured to the one behind him without really seeing anything. 'To the right the Eiffel Tower, to the left Notre Dame.'

'Actually, that's Hôtel de Ville to the left. You cannot see Notre Dame from that window.' She regarded him steadily. 'Have you ever actually walked around Paris before, Wolfe?'

'Sure. I've strolled from the airport to the car and from the car to whatever building I needed to enter.'

'Well, that at least explains why you don't understand my need to reconnect with the city,' she said. 'I might not be back here for some time and I want to wander up through Montmartre to Sacré Coeur, have lunch, and check out the new installation in my gallery before it is disassembled.'

'You agreed to let *me* decide when you could visit your gallery.'

'I've changed my mind.'

'You're angry because I'm calling the shots.'

'That has nothing to do with it. Did you have fun last night?'

The unexpected question threw him, and he watched through narrowed eyes as she rose and slowly approached the bed, gripping the bedpost in a provocative pose he wasn't even sure she was aware of.

'I can fit in Sacré Coeur, but you're not walking around Montmarte and your gallery is off-limits until I say so.'

He had leaked a fake itinerary to a couple of key suspects and the one she had devised for herself came too perilously close to it for comfort. Letting her have her way would put her in danger, and he couldn't live with himself if something happened to her. If she should—

'Look at you,' she said testily, her knuckles white where she gripped the bedpost. 'You are frustrated and angry with me and yet you won't show it. So controlled. So cool under pressure. Maybe the rumours are true and you *are* made out of ice.'

She turned, flicking her hair back over one shoulder in a quintessentially feminine gesture that dared a man to follow through with his baser instincts. Wolfe was not in the mood to let such a direct challenge go uncontested.

Within seconds he was on her, the flat of his hand slamming loudly against the wardrobe door as she was about to open it. 'You think I'm made out of ice, Princess? How quickly you forget.'

She spun around, her eyes wide, her breaths punching the air. Was that fear or anticipation he read in her dilated pupils?

He looked at her. At the silvery striations in her dark eyes and the tiny row of freckles that lined one side of her upper lip. Unable to help himself, he slid a hand into her hair and tilted her face up to his. Their eyes clashed in a battle of wills. He told himself to back off, settle down, but his gaze dropped to her soft mouth and he couldn't think of anything else but kissing her. Taking her.

Her nostrils flared as if sensing his need, and instead of crushing her lips beneath his he lightly brushed against them.

Once.

Twice.

She moaned and tried to draw his tongue into her mouth, but he'd thought about kissing her like this for weeks and now he didn't want to be rushed. He slipped his other arm around her waist and drew her against him, all the while teasing her lips with his. She twisted in his hold, her mouth moving beneath his as if she was as desperate for the contact as he was. As if she'd thought about this as often as he had. His hands swept over her back, cupping her firm butt and bringing her in closer against his pulsing hardness.

Her own hands were just as busy, roaming his chest, curving around his shoulders, burning him wherever she touched.

The sensation of her velvet tongue flicking against his threatened to drive him to his knees, and he pressed her against the wardrobe and wedged his leg between her thighs to keep them both upright. Her head thudded lightly against the wardrobe door and he cupped the nape of her neck and urged her mouth to open wider. She was like molten silk in his arms, sliding against him, urging him on with her husky whimpers for more.

Wolfe had felt his control slipping the moment he walked into the room. Now he had none. Even the thin barrier of their clothes was too much between them, and his hands stroked over her, shifting the slippery fabric aside as he sought the sweet perfection of her breasts.

For God only knew how long he was lost. A slave to sensation. A slave to her soft scent and even softer body. A slave to her heat, to the tug of her feminine fingers in his hair. If there was some reason he shouldn't be doing this he couldn't think of it.

Behind him he heard the snick of the latch as the door was quietly opened.

Thrusting Ava behind him he spun, his gun drawn, but even as he did so he knew he was at least two seconds too late.

The maid gasped softly and nearly fainted, but other than the sound of his own ragged breathing you could have heard a feather float to the floor.

So much for not making any more mistakes, Ice.

Hell.

If he needed a clearer example of just how poorly he was doing at the job of protecting her he didn't want to know what it was.

Wolfe stood motionless at the back of yet another extravagant ballroom and knew that despite donning yet another squillion-dollar tux he was doing nothing to blend into the glitterati of Paris. He was too angry with himself to care.

He should never have kissed her.

Now it was not only uncomfortable to watch her in the arms of another man, it was downright impossible. How his father had taken his mother back time after time Wolfe didn't know. He only knew he couldn't do it. If Ava chose someone else—Lorenzo—then she could have him.

Hell.

Of *course* she was going to choose someone else. That was the whole point of these elaborate tea parties and gala events. She was husband hunting and he thanked God he wasn't on her list.

Didn't he?

Of course he did. Even posing that question was a sign that he needed to step back. A very long way back.

And he would. In fact he already had. In—he checked his watch—fifteen minutes everything would have changed for the better. He blew out a long breath and dragged in some perspective with his next inhalation.

He knew how it felt to feel that someone you loved didn't love you, and… Oh, hell. He couldn't keep thinking like this. It felt as if his precious rules were in tatters, and he'd already thought and spoken more about his past in the last week than he had in twenty years. Next he'd be imagining that lust was love, and then where would he be? Hung out to dry like his old man, that was where. Talk about perspective.

It was a cliché that the client often fell for the bodyguard. It was just a hot mess if the opposite occurred, and he *fixed* hot messes—he didn't create them.

Telling himself she was just like any another woman wasn't working either. He wanted *her*. Not just any woman. *Her*.

When he had taken this gig his arrogant fat head had led him to believe he could control himself around her. *Yeah, right.* He'd proved in her hotel room two hours ago that he showed about as much control around her as a shark in a blood bath.

As a special ops soldier he had been trained to dig deep when every bone, muscle and tendon in his body was screaming for rest. He was trained to hold his line under extreme forms of torture no man should ever have to face. Apparently they hadn't thought to train him to resist desire of this magnitude. Of course in reality he *could* resist her—there was simply some part of him that didn't want to. And that was the part that scared him the most.

Ten minutes.

He shifted his weight to the balls of his feet and searched the baroque-style ballroom for her. She wasn't hard to find in that showstopper of swirling scarlet that hugged every inch of her lush curves—those it managed to contain anyway. If she'd wanted to make a statement of availability she'd succeeded. And Lorenzo was in the market and had the correct weight to buy.

But not Wolfe. His life was mapped out just as surely as hers. Work, women and play—in that order. It was a great life. A life any man with his head screwed on right would envy. A life he had never questioned before and, dammit, still didn't. That soft, sexy sound she made every time he slipped his tongue into her mouth was nothing he wouldn't forget with time.

Raucous laughter from somewhere behind him brought him out of his daze. Where the hell was she? The ever-moving crowd kept blocking his view, but even so his sixth sense told him she wasn't there.

An icy chill slid down his spine.

Glancing to the left, he caught the eye of one of his team acting as a waiter. Jonesy subtly signalled towards the patio doors leading to the gardens. His mouth tightened. He'd told her not to leave the room. No doubt the perfect Prince of Triole had taken her outside, and that wasn't going to happen on *his* watch.

Furious with himself for yet another lapse in concentration, Wolfe wove a determined line through the throng of guests until he was outside. Giving his eyes a moment to adjust to the dim light, he strained his hearing for the sound of her voice. Then he saw the flash of her strapless gown through the trees and the matching red stripe down the side of the Prince's trousers. His and hers. Perfection in the making, he thought acidly.

Lorenzo had caught her hands in his, the expression on his face one of earnest concentration. Was he about to propose? Wolfe didn't wait to find out.

'Nice night for a stroll, *ma'am*.'

Ava stiffened at the sound of Wolfe's voice behind her and tugged her hands out of Lorenzo's. She knew Wolfe was reprimanding her for going against his orders, but she didn't care. Since he'd walked out of her hotel room she'd been more determined than ever to find Lorenzo attractive. She didn't want Wolfe to be the only man who could make her melt with mindless passion, because she knew he was determined to stay unattached for ever and she needed the opposite. She *wanted* the opposite! And wanting something more with him was just asking for heartache. Especially when the look on his face as he'd stormed out of her hotel room had left her in no doubt as to how appalled he was by the attraction that still simmered between them.

He moved now, blocking her way, his legs set wide apart, his hands clasped behind his back. He was so intensely male he took her breath away and, try as she had all night, she couldn't forget the way it felt to be pressed up against all that hard muscle.

Previously she would have said she wasn't a woman who could get turned on by a powerful man. But of course previously she hadn't met Wolfe. Hadn't felt this explosion of chemistry that made her tingle and burn. Hadn't felt such a strong need to be with someone not just sexually but…always.

She let out a silent, shaky breath she hoped he wouldn't notice and stared him down.

'Prince Lorenzo and I would like some privacy, Wolfe.'

'I need to talk to you.'

Ava shook her head. Talking was a bad idea. Forgetting about what had happened in her hotel room was what was required. 'Not now.'

Wolfe cut his eyes to Lorenzo and she knew he was on the verge of ordering him to leave. Only Wolfe would consider doing that with a man who was second in line to the throne.

'Wolfe, please.' She hated the way she sounded as if she was begging but she was. She couldn't do this any more. First thing tomorrow morning she was going to contact her father and tell him to organise another bodyguard. Wolfe could still head up the case if he liked, but she knew there was absolutely no way she could feel anything more than friendship for any man she met while Wolfe was by her side. Even when he wasn't with her she thought of him, ached for him. She was starting to fear that no one would measure up to him. *Ever.*

His jaw clenched, as it always did when he was annoyed with her, and if possible his expression grew even more remote.

God, he was impossible! That kiss back in her hotel room… Her lips parted…

Don't think about it, she ordered herself.

Not easy when he blocked her path, giving her no choice but to either wait for him to step aside or turn around with her tail tucked between her legs and retreat back inside as he wanted her to do.

Ava knew which option she *wasn't* going to take.

Stepping closer to him was a mistake, though, as her senses became immediately overloaded with the faint trace of musk and man—a combination that instantly flooded her body with heat and need.

She shivered and Lorenzo placed his hand on her shoulder. Straight away her undisciplined mind compared its size and texture to Wolfe's. It felt cool, where Wolfe's always felt so warm it bordered on hot, and it didn't make her want to wind herself around him until she didn't know where she ended and he began.

'Are you cold, *piccolina*?'

For a minute Ava thought Wolfe might do Lorenzo damage, and she quickly smiled her reassurance at Lorenzo before throwing Wolfe a baleful stare. 'We can talk later. Right now I need you to move out of my way.'

In more ways than one, her mind quipped unhelpfully.

Ava waited, remembering the time he had threatened to toss her onto his horse. Back then she hadn't believed he'd really do it. Now she knew better. Wolfe always got the job done, no matter what.

He glanced at his watch and then stepped aside, but it didn't feel as if she had won a major victory.

In a fit of frustration she tightened her hold on Lorenzo's arm in an attempt to disconnect her senses from Wolfe.

Oh, who was she kidding? She'd done it to send a message to Wolfe that his rejection of her hadn't affected her in the slightest. That she didn't *need* him. But silently she accepted that if Lucy hadn't interrupted them they'd have made love again. And she couldn't dislodge the sensation that it just felt so right to be in Wolfe's arms.

'Ava?'

'I'm sorry, Lorenzo. I was…you were telling me about how we could integrate the telecommunications networks between Anders and Triole?'

Ava let him fill her head with possibilities and murmured appropriately, but her heart wasn't in it and, feeling Wolfe's steely silence behind her, she experienced an overwhelming need to escape both men and take stock. And she would have done exactly that if Wolfe hadn't cleared his throat and stepped forwards again.

'Ma'am.' His voice was dark and official. 'We need to have that talk now.'

Ava glanced from Wolfe to the burly man in an expensive suit and with a grim expression standing beside him. Did he have news about her situation?

Excusing herself from Lorenzo, Ava waited for Wolfe to speak.

'Ma'am, this is Dan Rogers. He's a security specialist who has worked for me for a number of years. He'll be taking over your security detail from now on.'

It took a minute for Wolfe's words to sink in, and when they did Ava's stomach bottomed out. 'You're quitting?' She couldn't believe it. He'd told her he would *never* quit, and she realised with a start that she'd come to rely on that.

'Not quitting. I'm rearranging the team to better utilise our skill-set.'

Ava heard what he said but she didn't believe it. This wasn't about skill-sets. This was about that kiss in her hotel room.

With her thoughts and feelings swirling around inside her like leaves in a whirly wind, she said the first thing that came to mind. 'My father won't like it.'

Wolfe's jaw clenched and released. 'I'll deal with your father.'

Before she could think of anything else except the sick feeling growing in the pit of her stomach he turned to the other man.

'Take care of her. Once she's secure for the night call me and I'll come and give you a complete brief.'

The man nodded.

Wolfe nodded and then turned his eyes briefly to hers. 'Goodbye…ma'am.'

Ava closed her eyes and leant her head back against the butter-soft leather seats inside her limousine. She was alone in the car, having forbidden her new bodyguard from riding with her. He hadn't liked it, but she'd given him the super-special superior look that had never worked on Wolfe and he'd acquiesced.

Now she felt horribly alone and hankered for something familiar. Something to anchor her in a world that kept moving and changing at a pace she was struggling to keep up with. She'd had so many decisions to make lately she was completely exhausted. No wonder she felt so out of sorts. Life-changes usually happened one at a time and with some sense of order. Didn't they? At least that had been her experience to date. But these past few weeks nothing had been as it should. Least of all her.

In a split-second decision she knew Wolfe would call a

'spontaneous reaction' Ava instructed the driver to take her to her gallery, and immediately felt better.

The restless energy flowing through her was somewhat appeased at the thought of seeing Monique's new works. They'd been installed two weeks ago, and viewing them on her smartphone wasn't the same as standing back and inspecting them in person.

She smiled as her change in plans was relayed to the other two cars. No doubt Wolfe would have a kitten…but he had chosen to abandon his post and there was nothing he could do about it. She imagined the conversation they might have if he were here. Was it wrong to enjoy their mental tussles with each other so much?

When the car stopped Ava didn't wait for her chauffeur to open her door but did it herself, breathing in the sweet damp air of Place des Vosges.

Her new bodyguard stopped beside her. 'Ma'am, I'd like you to wait a few minutes before heading inside.'

Ava considered that briefly and then realised why. 'Is Wolfe on his way?'

'Yes, ma'am.'

Ava cursed. 'I thought you were in charge now?'

'I am. However—'

'Never mind. And, no, I won't wait for your boss to join us.'

Pivoting on her heel, she set off across the square to the row of shops she knew like the back of her hand. Her footsteps echoed in the quiet night that was only broken by the low hum of fast-moving cars on the main road and the squeak and clunk of a garbage truck as it rattled along the cobbled streets.

Dan reached the solid metal door to her building before her and held his hand out for the key. 'I'll do that, ma'am.'

A car door slammed somewhere close behind her but she ignored it.

'I can do it.' It might be the last time she ever did, and she wanted to take in every moment.

'Ava!'

Wolfe's hard, angry voice made her fingers fumble the key, and that made her mad. He wasn't going to ruin this for her by muscling his way in. She wouldn't let him.

Of course her stupid key chose that moment to become stuck and, frustrated, she twisted it in the opposite direction. Wolfe's harsh, 'Get back!' confused her, and then a strong arm wrapped around her middle and yanked her sideways seconds before a deafening bang exploded in her ear.

CHAPTER NINE

SHE SCREAMED AND then lost her breath as she felt as if a giant boulder had fallen on top of her.

'Secure…the…area.'

Wolfe's deep voice, laden with pain, instructed the men running towards them. Ava coughed as she tried to breathe the filthy air around them, but her lungs were constricted. Feeling winded, she tried to twist onto her back and realised that it was Wolfe who was smothering her with his body.

When he shifted she dragged in a bucketload of acrid-smelling air. 'What…?'

'Ava. Don't move.' Deft hands ran over her body with mechanical efficiency, and when he was satisfied she wasn't seriously injured he hovered over her, his movements somehow lacking their usual fluid grace.

Hearing a ringing sound in her ears, she peered around to see that the front of her building was completely blown apart. The fire door she had installed as a precaution lay crumpled as if a giant fist had tried to punch holes in it.

Bewildered by the chaos and devastation around her, and only peripherally aware that Wolfe's men surrounded them, Ava glanced at Wolfe. '*Mon Dieu*, you are hurt.'

Ignoring the pain in her hands and hip where she had hit the pavement, she reached out to the jagged tear down the sleeve of his jacket. The white shirt beneath was already turning crimson under the glow of the street lamp that remained intact like a silent sentinel above them.

'Get her…into the car,' Wolfe rasped, shrugging out of his torn jacket.

'No.' Ava tried to reach for him, her only thought to help him, but he slashed his hand in the air.

'Now.'

His voice brooked no argument and before she could do anything his men had gripped her arms and steered her back towards the limousine. She could hear Wolfe ruthlessly issuing orders and the distant wail of a police siren. Concerned voices filtered through the dust and smoke and then faded away as Wolfe's men held back any curious onlookers drawn by the explosion.

Within minutes of the police arriving Wolfe was beside her in the car, wearing a black leather jacket; nothing about his appearance suggested that he'd just thrown himself on top of her as a bomb had blasted glass, bricks and plaster all over him.

He seemed calm and eerily controlled.

By contrast Ava couldn't stop trembling. She was to blame for what had happened. Wolfe had told her not to change her itinerary and she hadn't listened. She had wanted—what? The comfort of the familiar? To get back at Wolfe for leaving her? To make him come after her?

She let out a shaky breath. Right now all she knew was that she had put those assigned to take care of her in danger and she felt awful.

On top of all that the threat to her life was obviously real! Somehow she had held on to the notion that Wolfe was wrong. But it wasn't he who had been wrong, it was her.

'I'm sorry,' she whispered helplessly. 'I feel terrible.'

'It's not your fault.' His voice was clipped, withdrawn. It made her feel worse because she could tell he was blaming himself.

Tears welled behind her eyes but she told herself not to get emotional. That now was not the time. But emotion was stronger than logic even on a good day. 'That is nonsense. I should have—'

'No! *I* should have.' His eyes met hers and he stopped. 'Where are you hurt?'

'I'm okay.'

'Ava.' The way he said her name was a warning that he was going to go completely macho if she didn't cooperate, but all she could think about was how much she loved the way it sounded on his lips.

'My wrist.' And her hip. And she could really use a glass of water.

As if she'd spoken out loud he retrieved a bottle from the mini-bar and untwisted the top.

'Merci.'

After she'd finished he took the bottle. 'Give me a look at your hands.'

Shaking, Ava held them out and he gently felt along her wristbones. She winced as he pressed on her tender palm, but he continued his inspection undeterred.

'I don't think bones are broken, but your palms are badly scraped.'

'They'll heal,' she dismissed, catching his brooding frown.

'Thankfully.'

His phone rang before she could ask what would happen next and he released her hand to answer it.

She closed her eyes as the night-dark city whisked by. Wolfe didn't try to touch her or talk to her again but she wanted him to. She felt chilled, as if she'd never be warm again. And for once she didn't argue when he took complete control of the situation. Right now it was easier to sit back and let him do what he did best.

She stole a glance at his austere profile. His jaw was packed with tension, his expression tough. He would do anything to keep her safe because he *had* to, and all she wanted was for him to do it because he *wanted* to.

With a start she realised just how much she trusted him to take care of her. How much she trusted him to have her best interests at heart.

'Please don't be angry at Dan,' she said, suddenly realising that she might have put the other man's job at risk. 'He tried to stop me.'

'I'm not angry at Dan,' he said flatly.

No. He was angry with her. With himself, perhaps.

'You won't fire him?'

'Your concern for his future is a little misplaced. Your behaviour tonight could have got him killed. It could have got you— Hell! What were you thinking?'

Although his words were angry his tone sounded more… devastated. And that sent her own sense of guilt higher.

'I wanted…something familiar. Closure.'

'Closure?'

'I felt restless after you left and I knew I wouldn't sleep. It seemed like a good idea.'

He shook his head. 'I should have told Dan to physically waylay you.'

'Why didn't you?'

His gaze was intense when it connected with hers. 'I didn't want him touching you.'

Ava swallowed at the raw admission.

'Just another mistake on my part.' He blew out a breath and turned away from her, his hands knotted into fists on his thighs.

'Do you think any of Monique's paintings survived?'

He looked at her as if she'd grown another head, but then his expression softened. 'Unlikely. Your fire door sent most of the explosion inward instead of outward. It tells me that whoever set it was more rank amateur than stalwart professional.'

'Do you have any idea who it might be?'

'If I did I'd have my hands around their throat right now.'

'Me, too.'

He shook his head at her, a reluctant smile forming on his lips. 'You are one tough lady, Princess.'

Ava's nose crinkled. She wasn't great at accepting praise even when she felt like she deserved it, but she couldn't deny the warm glow Wolfe's words lit up inside her.

When the car stopped it was a good excuse to refocus her thoughts. Glancing outside, she could see they were on some form of airstrip, but it was too dark to make out exactly where they were. The only source of light was coming from the open rectangular door of Wolfe's private plane.

Wolfe waited for his men to flank the car before opening the door. He glanced around, his eyes scanning the darkness. He was so fierce. So sure. He braced himself against the car as he leant down and beckoned to her. 'This way.'

Careful of her injured palms, Ava scooted across the soft leather, still warm from his body. The softly falling rain chilled her bare shoulders and arms as she stepped out of the car.

Immediately Wolfe moved into her space and lifted her into his arms.

'I can walk.'

'My way is quicker.'

His tone told her he was readying himself for an argument, but frankly Ava didn't have the energy and wasn't sure of how capable she was of making it up the steps under her own steam anyway.

She sighed and rested her head against his chest, her eyelids too heavy to stay propped open. No doubt he was taking her back to Anders, but she'd much prefer a tropical island far away from the outside world if she was given the choice.

Once on his plane she kept her eyes closed, and only opened them when she felt Wolfe gently lower her onto a soft mattress.

The doctor Wolfe had sent to her at Gilles's was waiting and Ava struggled to a sitting position, with the reams of fabric from her torn and dirty gown twisting around her legs.

He followed Wolfe's instructions and checked her wrist-bones before efficiently sticking a number of plasters over her scraped palms. 'These will feel stiff and sore for a couple of days, due to the bruising beneath the scratches, but they should heal fine.'

'Check her left hip. It's bothering her.'

Her eyes flew to his. How did he know it hurt? 'It's fine.'

'Check it.'

Ava only flinched once during his gentle ministrations, grateful when he deemed it only a light bruise.

'What about you?' She glanced at Wolfe but he was busy checking an incoming message on his phone.

'I'm fine. Thanks, Jock. Tell Stevens to get us airborne as quickly as possible.'

It was only after he said it that Ava became conscious of the whine of the aircraft. Seconds later they were racing towards the sky.

Her eyes traced the smudges of dust covering Wolfe's sandy-blond hair and moved down over his snowy-white shirt beneath the leather jacket.

'You're shivering. Here.' Wolfe pulled a brand-new white shirt out of a small closet, his movements as clipped as his tone. 'I don't have anything for you to wear and both your clothes and your lady's maid are back at the hotel. Can you get changed yourself?'

'Into a shirt?'

'It's all I have here.'

Ava stared at it, the events of the night crashing in around her. Tears pricked behind her eyes and she bit her bottom lip. Hard. She felt scarily vulnerable and needy. The feeling brought both Frédéric's and her mother's death into sharp focus inside her mind.

'Come here,' he said gently.

Wolfe gripped her shoulders, but Ava was afraid if she gave in to the comfort he was offering she would break down completely and never let him go. She shook her head. 'I need to use the bathroom. I'm filthy.'

He looked as if he wanted to argue but then released her. 'Bathroom's through there.'

As the enormity of what had happened hit her full-on Ava had to concentrate to make her legs carry her the short distance across the plane.

Once inside the pristine bathroom, she used the amenities and eyed the shower stall despondently. It would take too long to shower with her hands bandaged, but she would love to just wash the night away if she could.

Don't think about it, she ordered herself. *Then maybe it will all go away.*

She felt like crying.

Reaching around to the side of her gown, she let out an impatient growl as her clumsy fingers fought to drag the zipper down. Then she heard the unmistakable sound of fabric tearing and a sob rose in her throat. The once beautiful gown sagged and fell to the floor and it took all her effort to remain standing. Crying over a dress when someone was trying to kill her...when someone had killed her brother... Pathetic.

Telling herself to get a grip, she kicked off her heels and stuffed her arms into Wolfe's shirt. She knew immediately by the linen smell that he'd never worn it, and that made her want to cry even more.

Dashing at her useless tears to hold them back, she nearly screamed aloud when she couldn't even do the simple task of sliding buttons into buttonholes. Her fingers were hampered by the thick bandages and the length of the shirtsleeves that dangled past her wrists and refused to stay pushed up her arms.

'Oh, damn, damn, *damn.*'

'Ava? Are you okay in there?'

Ava stopped cursing and stilled. '*Oui*. Fine.'

The door opened regardless and Wolfe stood framed in the doorway, with his hands on his hips. He'd changed into a clean shirt that hung out over soft denim jeans. *Magnificent* didn't even begin to describe him.

Wolfe felt as if someone had just tried to squeeze every drop of blood out of his heart as he took in the sight of her standing in the middle of the bathroom, pale and regal, clutching the sides of his shirt together, her torn gown like a puddle of blood circling her bare legs and feet. Tear-marks tracked down her dirty face and her lower lip was trembling as she tried to hold herself together.

He'd never met another woman like her. One who faced life's challenges with grit and determination. One who wasn't afraid to face the truth about herself and, when she set her mind to something, just gathered her courage, rolled up her sleeves and got on with it.

Something tugged in the region of his heart. She was beautiful and strong and...*special*. The word anchored inside his mind and wouldn't budge. It didn't help that she looked as sexy as hell in his shirt.

'I can't do up these damned buttons,' she complained, her voice rough as she worked to hold back tears, her brow furrowed.

'Oh, baby...' Wolfe didn't have a lot of experience dealing with female tears but he acted purely on instinct as he stepped into the room and closed his arms around her. Something satisfying was released inside him when she buried her head against his chest and sniffed. It felt as if she belonged there, but he immediately dismissed the rogue thought. That kind of thinking was totally against his rules.

Her arms slid around his back and he ignored the bolt of discomfort that shot up his spine as she inadvertently touched muscles that had been crushed when part of the wall of her gallery building had landed on top of him.

'Do you know why I chose Paris?'

Her soft voice was muffled against his shirt front and she reminded him of the bunch of newborn kittens he and his brother had once found abandoned in one of the back sheds on their farm. He and Adam had secretly fed them until they had grown too big to be contained. His father had wanted to drown the lot of them, but both of them had begged him to reconsider. Then they had made signs and taken the kittens to the local mall, and stayed all day until the last one had been given away.

The stupid memory made him feel suddenly vulnerable, and he cleared his throat and smoothed his hand up and down Ava's back to distract himself. 'No. Why?'

'It's my mother's city. She grew up here. After she died my life became like something out of a Dickens novel. My father didn't know how to deal with a teenage daughter so he didn't. Since Frédéric had been sent to military school, I…I…'

'You had no one.'

'No.'

A raw sob ripped from her throat and, remembering her stoic reaction to the news of Frédéric's death, Wolfe guessed that she had probably never let herself grieve the loss. The futile destruction of her gallery would be just one more injury for her to try to cope with.

The need to comfort her overrode any sense of self-preservation he had left. Gathering her close, he cradled the back of her head and soaked up her tears, absorbing as much of her pain as he could. When the storm had passed she shifted even closer and every muscle in his body tensed in response.

'You must think I'm a weak foo— Oh, my God. Why did you not tell me I looked like this?'

Wolfe glanced over his shoulder and saw her horrified

reflection in the small bathroom mirror. He eased her away from him and pushed her mass of hair back from her face. 'Really? I thought you were just going for the Panda of the Year award.'

'Yes. With dreadlocks,' she scoffed, dashing at the dusty tear-smudges on her cheeks with the back of one hand. The other was holding her shirt blessedly closed.

'Here, let me.' Still taking most of her weight, and trying not to think about how good she felt leaning into him, Wolfe reached around her and wet a facecloth with warm water. He tilted her chin up and gently wiped as much of the grit and smudges from her face as he could. His muscles knotted as he thought of how close she had come to dying, but he forced himself to relax. Right now her needs took precedence over his rage.

She must have sensed the change in him because she gave him a half-hearted smile and started fumbling with the tiny buttons on his shirt.

Damn, he was going to have to do that for her, as well.

Gently knocking her hands aside, he reached for the top button of the shirt. 'Let me do that. It will be quicker.'

Her beautiful red-rimmed eyes met his and sweat broke out on his forehead. He needed to think of something else.

First, remove the dust cover, then release the tension on the recoil spring.

Okay, he started disassembling an AK47 in his head. That was definitely something else.

His fingers felt feeble as he forced the buttons into their holes and he paused when he accidentally brushed the sweet-smelling skin between her breasts.

Slide the hammer back.

What the hell were these buttons made of anyway? Plasticine?

Gas tube off—

No, idiot. Adjust the front sight post first.

Oh, what the hell.

There was no way cold hard metal could compete with the memory of the weight of those round breasts in the palm of his hands and he gave up, giving his mind permission to conjure up the bumpy texture of her nipples when they were aroused into tight peaks, their colour, their flavour…

Finally reaching the last button, and completely disgusted with himself, Wolfe was glad he didn't have that useless AK47 handy or he might shoot himself with it. He'd been as good as useless to her tonight anyway.

With professional detachment he ignored the question in his head about whether she was wearing panties and lifted her into his arms, hoping to God she couldn't feel his thundering heartbeat. He strode into the plane's bedroom and placed her quickly on the turned-back bed.

About to tell her he'd leave her to rest, he realised she hadn't moved, but sat huddled right where he'd put her.

'Ava…' He said her name on an exhalation. She looked so washed-out and unhappy he couldn't stop himself from placing his knee on the bed beside her and rubbing his hands over her shoulders. 'Baby, lie down.'

She shook her head and her lower lip wobbled again.

'Come on, Princess. Time for sleep.'

He eased her down on the pillows and smoothed her hair back from her face, determined to let that be the end of it.

'Wolfe?' Her voice, barely a whisper, was laced with fatigue and shock. 'Could you stay with me? I mean…just for a minute.'

Could he stay with her? Sure. *Should* he stay with her? No.

Wolfe closed his eyes and held himself still. It would be a monumental mistake to say yes. He wanted to stay. All too much. Which was why he shouldn't.

'Okay.' His hand slipped to the side of her face, caressing the cool skin of her cheek, her jaw. Before he had time to think about it he eased in beside her and leaned his back against the headboard. Without a word he gathered her close and felt her whole body sigh as she arranged her limbs to slot perfectly against his own—as if he'd been made specifically for this purpose. Specifically for her.

A sensation of warmth spread inside his chest and a lump formed in his throat. Without being truly conscious of it he stroked her back. 'Sleep, Princess. I'll be here.'

Had he really just promised that?

After promising himself he'd keep as much physical distance from her as possible?

Well, yes, but there was time to re-implement that plan once he had her on his island. His house wasn't huge, but it was big enough to get lost in, and once he had her safe he'd be able to lock himself away and get to work.

So, yes, he would stay for now, give her the comfort she had sought and failed to receive as a lonely teenager, and then he'd get up. Pore over the intel his team would have sent him about the bomb. He had a suspicion he knew who was behind the attack on her life, given the people he had deliberately leaked Ava's bogus itinerary to, and it was time to find out if his instincts were correct.

Releasing a slow breath, he willed his pain-racked body to fake relaxation. Earlier, when he had spotted Ava in front of her building it had been like running over moon grass instead of smooth pavement trying to reach her. His instincts had been screaming that he should have sent somebody over to check the gallery earlier that night. He hadn't—another slip-up—and he'd nearly lost her. Hell, a newly minted grunt could do a better job of protecting her than he had.

She made a light snuffling sound in her sleep and he realised he'd been stroking her hair. He untangled his fingers and pulled his hand back, wincing when a strand caught in one of his chipped fingernails.

Seriously, it was time to stop mooning over those blue,

blue eyes and the honeyed taste of her mouth and remember she wasn't a goddamned date.

He cursed low under his breath as he realised he'd given himself this same pep talk once before. Then it had been as effective as trying to milk a cow while wearing gardening gloves. Something else he and his brother had tried once. And what was with all these childhood memories streaming into his consciousness as silent and insidious as floodwater?

His gaze slid to Ava's face. A soft wave of her hair had fallen across her cheek and he gently moved it back. The lump in his throat returned with interest.

Dammit, he had to pull back. If he didn't do white picket fences he certainly didn't do bluestone rock with a moat and a drawbridge! But there was nothing he could do to stem the flood of feeling her near-death had opened up in him. He'd do anything to protect her. He knew it. And it was only sensible that he hated that feeling.

About to move off the bed, he felt her arm stretch and settle across his waist. Helpless to do anything else, Wolfe watched her sleep.

CHAPTER TEN

AVA HADN'T HAD any time to feel embarrassed over her crying stint. Once they'd landed Wolfe had hustled her from the plane and led her to a waiting Jeep. She knew instantly that they weren't in Anders, where she had assumed he had been taking her. It was the humid night heat and the smell of eucalyptus in the air.

'Where are we?'

Wolfe stopped beside the black Jeep. 'An island.'

Ava gave a short laugh. 'You're kidding?'

'No. Why?'

She shook her head, wondering if she was still dreaming. 'No reason.' She knew she must have been dreaming that Wolfe had sat with her during the whole flight and stroked her hair. Ava hesitated before preceding him into the car. 'Which island?'

'Cape Paraiso. It's a small private island off the west coast of Africa.'

She studied the carved planes of his profile in the starry sky, noting the sense of ownership in his voice. 'Yours?'

'It was on sale. Get in.'

Ava already knew that Wolfe hadn't grown up wealthy, which meant he was a self-made man, and she couldn't help but like how unassuming he was about his success.

She stifled a yawn as the car zoomed along a rough track.

She gingerly held on to the door to stop herself from sliding against Wolfe's solid frame, but he didn't even notice as he scrolled through some sort of document on his phone.

'Do you have any ideas as to who is responsible yet?'

He glanced at her briefly, his expression guarded. 'I'm working around the clock on it.'

Ava let him read. The wind was up and it rustled through towering hardwood trees. The glint of the moon shone silvery streaks on the inky ocean. She could just make out a solid stone house that looked to be set into the side of a cliff, and as they drove closer she saw that it was finished with a tiled roof and acres of glass.

When the car had pulled into a short circular driveway Wolfe jumped stiffly from the Jeep. Her eyes followed him as he walked around the front of the car. If she wasn't mistaken he was very much a man in pain. She remembered the blood on his torn jacket before he'd changed out of it and reluctantly acknowledged that she had become so absorbed in the horror of what had happened she hadn't thought about his injuries at all.

Wolfe hovered by her side.

'I'm okay. I can walk.'

After a brief pause he nodded. 'Follow me.'

The tiles were cool and slightly gritty with sand beneath her bare feet, but Ava had only a moment to admire the massive front door before she was inside a foyer-cum-living area that could comfortably house his plane and the Jeep and still have room to spare for an ocean liner.

'Wow!'

'You like it?'

Ava glanced at him. 'It's enormous.'

'The size is deceptive. This is the largest area because of the aspect. Are you hungry?'

Her hand went to her belly and she shook her head. 'I couldn't eat anything.'

He nodded. 'I'll take you to your room.'

She followed him along the narrow hallway.

'This corridor leads to the bedroom. The other one leads into the kitchen, gym and pool area. The house is all on one level so I doubt you'll get lost.'

He led her down a long hallway that had various other hallways leading off it and she wondered absently if they shared the same idea of size. 'Is it just us?'

He stopped outside a closed door and threw it open. 'Yes. The island is completely private. The couple who caretake for me live on a larger island about an hour away. Wait here.'

He stepped into the room, flicked on the light and checked the double glass doors leading to an outdoor area. When his gaze returned to her she became intensely aware that she was standing in the middle of a bedroom wearing nothing more than one of his shirts and a teensy pair of knickers. Every cell in her body seemed to vibrate on high alert and she wondered if he was at all affected by her. On some level she knew he had to be, but he was so good at controlling himself. It made her want to rip her shirt open and push all that stony self-control to the limit.

'I don't have any women's clothing and I can't send out for any. That shirt should do you tonight. In the morning I'll lend you some T-shirts and shorts of mine.'

'Merci.'

'I'd also prefer you didn't go outside. The whole house is alarmed and I don't want you tripping it.'

Without waiting for her acquiescence he strode to the door. 'You should have everything you need in the *en suite* bathroom, but I will be next door if you should need anything else.'

Like him?

The impulsive thought jumped into her mind and she smiled brightly. 'I'm sure I'll be fine.'

Or at least she wouldn't tell him if she wasn't.

Wolfe nodded. 'Goodnight then.'

Feeling wired after her rest on the plane, Ava turned her interested gaze to the room. It was large and airy and continued the strong Spanish feel of the other rooms, with terracotta floors inlaid with handcrafted mosaics, brightly coloured rugs and light timber furniture.

She'd dearly love to take a shower, but that seemed impossible with her bandaged hands. Nor could she go outside. Glancing around the stylishly furnished room she found nothing to distract herself, not even a TV.

With nothing to do she freshened up in the bathroom as best she could with her cumbersome bandages and lay down on the comfortable bed, willing herself to sleep again. Her mother had always said she could do anything if she put her mind to it, but it seemed that sleep on command wasn't one of those achievements.

Thinking of her mother made her feel sad again. Sad and alone. She had been the only person who understood her need to shine in her own right. Her need to stand on her own two feet.

Wolfe understands you.

The sneaky little thought crept sideways into her brain and transported her back to the bed on his plane. Rolling sideways, she shifted restlessly and felt bereft in the empty bed. Snuggling into his big body had been… It had been… Ava felt her pelvis clench in response. Yes, it had been heavenly. He was so warm. So solid. And this bed in comparison was cold. Empty. Exactly how she felt right now.

What would he do if she went to him…naked? Would it matter that he would never love her the way she desperately wanted to be loved?

Irritated with herself, she rolled onto her back and stared at the dark ceiling. Why, oh, why couldn't she get that man out of her head?

And why couldn't Lorenzo affect her half as much? Marrying him would solve every one of her problems. He was the spare to the heir in his own country, so he understood the pressures she would face as Queen. And he was kind. Considerate. The perfect gentleman.

But she didn't love him and he didn't love her. Although it was possible that love would grow; it often did in arranged marriages.

And it often didn't either.

'Oh, shut up!' Ava told the insistent voice in her head.

She would have to sleep with him. Take him into her body. And that just felt…

Wrong.

'Yes, yes. I get it.'

And talking to an empty room wasn't going to change anything. Feeling horribly alone, and miserably vulnerable after the night's events, Ava felt a desperate urge to leave a message for her father. To reconnect with him in some small way. Something her mother would no doubt be immensely happy with.

About to reach for her phone, she realised she had no idea where it was. She knew she'd had it in the limousine on the way to her gallery because she'd ignored an incoming message. Or had that been during the dinner earlier? She couldn't remember, but no doubt if she had left it in either place one of Wolfe's efficient men would have picked it up for her.

If they had where would they have left it? The living room? The kitchen? No way would they come to her room and disturb her.

Mulling over her options, Ava decided to take a look; she knew she wouldn't sleep anyway, and maybe she would fix herself a glass of warm milk in the process.

Feeling marginally better now that she was taking action, she stepped out of her room, feeling a bit like a thief as her bare feet padded silently on the tiled floor.

Hoping she was headed in the right direction, she stopped

when she noticed a triangle of light spilling into the hallway ahead of her.

Wolfe obviously wasn't in bed yet. Or maybe it was the driver of the Jeep. Maybe he could help her.

Cautiously moving forward, she felt a sense of trepidation tightening her throat as every horror movie she had ever seen vied for supremacy in her head. She leaned around the open doorway and her hand flew to her mouth to stifle her shocked gasp.

Wolfe was standing in a small utility room, naked to the waist, his back covered in a crisscross pattern of fresh welts and bruises. A large medical kit stood open on the marble benchtop, bandages, scissors and blood-covered swabs strewn around it. A white gauze bandage he had clearly applied himself ran the length of his left triceps.

As if in a daze she connected her eyes with his in the wide mirror. 'Oh, my God. That looks terrible.'

When it had felt as if a wall had fallen on her it *had*, she realised, but Wolfe had taken the brunt of the impact. Broken pieces of brick, wood and plaster had turned his bronzed flesh into a checkerboard of pain. The shock of the night returned full force and, feeling sick to her stomach, Ava moved into the room.

Wolfe spun around, presenting her for the first time in weeks with the sight of his magnificent hair-roughened chest.

Ava barely noticed.

Her eyes slid past his impressive pectoral muscles to where his bruised back could be seen as clear as day under the fluorescent light.

'It looks worse than it is.'

Her eyes met his. 'I very much doubt that.' Her hand covered her mouth again. 'Wolfe, I am *so* sorry.'

Swearing softly under his breath, he reached for the shirt he'd dropped onto the floor.

'I told you it wasn't your fault.' The words were more like

a grunt, but he didn't move to cover himself with the T-shirt as she stepped into his personal space.

'Much.' She gave him a stilted smile. 'What is this cream for?' She picked up the opened jar on the vanity behind him and smelt it.

'It's arnica. It's a natural remedy that takes a lot of the pain out of bruises.'

'So you *do* feel pain?' She tried to make light of it to curb how truly awful she felt about his injuries.

'Not if I can help it,' he said flatly.

She cocked her eyebrow at him and noticed him stiffen when she dabbed her finger into the jar. 'Turn around,' she instructed on impulse.

He shook his head, swallowed heavily. 'I can take care of myself.'

Ava understood his need for self-sufficiency. On a much smaller scale she too had decided it was safer to rely only on herself, but for some reason she wanted Wolfe to know that she was there for him just as much as he had been there for her.

Finding it hard to maintain eye contact with him as he towered over her, Ava nevertheless held her ground. 'Everyone needs someone, Wolfe.'

'I don't.' His words sounded gritty. Empty.

'Yes, you do. You're just too afraid to admit it.' Ava twirled her finger. 'Now, turn around. Please,' she added when it looked as if he wouldn't comply.

He shook his head in mock resignation. 'Anyone ever tell you you're a bossy little thing?'

'Hmm, there was a man once who might have uttered something similar.'

'What happened to him?'

'I threw him in my dungeon.'

'Then I better not cross you,' he said gravely.

'A smart man.' She laughed. 'Who knew?'

He scowled at her but there was a twinkling of humour in his toffee eyes. Her breath caught as she took in his male beauty, but then he turned and she could barely stop herself from wincing when she saw his back again. 'Tell me if I hurt you.'

'You won't.'

Their eyes met briefly in the mirror and she knew he was right. If anyone was going to get hurt here it would be her.

Ignoring the maudlin thought, she concentrated on being gentle as she touched him.

She felt him tense up at her first touch. His hands braced against the vanity unit, but other than that he didn't move as she worked the cool cream into his discoloured skin. 'Weren't you wearing one of those special vests?' she asked to distract herself while she worked.

'Kevlar is better against bullets than bombs. Although it hurts like a son of a bitch to get shot.'

And she knew he knew what *that* felt like.

He was so strong, this warrior of a man who had shielded her so well all she'd ended up with was a bruised hip and sore hands.

Fortunately her plasters didn't hinder her fingers from spreading cream onto him, and by the time she'd worked her way down to the base of his spine she felt his muscles start to relax.

And then other sensations started to creep into her consciousness. Sensations like the fact that his warm, toned flesh was beneath her fingertips. Like his size. The fact that she was standing so closely behind him she would only have to move a centimetre to be plastered against all that heat.

Just like that lust unfurled like a flower low in her pelvis and turned her insides to liquid. She glanced at his face in the mirror and found his eyes were shut tight, his knuckles as white as the basin he gripped. It was as if he was holding on to his control by a thread. As if her touching him was affecting him the same way it was affecting her.

Without allowing herself any time to think about it, she leant forward and placed her lips along the indent of his spine, feeling rather than hearing his sharp inhalation. He smelt of soap and the cream now absorbed into his skin. And all man. Ava breathed deep, careful not to press against his bruises but unable to stop kissing him on every undamaged section of his back.

He was tall, so much taller than her, and she had to stretch to reach the base of his neck. As soon as her lips found their mark a deep sound rumbled through his body and he spun towards her, his hands gripping her waist to hold her back.

A tap dripped in the quiet room but neither of them paid it any attention.

Ava knew her eyes showed how aroused she was but she didn't try to hide it from him. She knew he would never want a future with her, but at this point she didn't care.

Last week she had pledged that she would dedicate her life to her country. But that seemed irrelevant tonight. Tonight they had both nearly lost their lives. Tonight she just wanted to be a normal woman with a man who made her feel so much.

'What are you doing, Ava?'

His deep growl sent a frisson of awareness straight to her core.

She spread her hands wide over his magnificent chest. 'What does it look like?'

'It looks like trouble.'

She smiled. 'I want to make love with you, Wolfe.'

His nostrils flared and his fingers bit into her waist. Like a sinuous cat Ava arched towards him, powered by the knowledge that he seemed to be as aroused as she already was.

When he continued to stare at her, unmoving, she wondered if perhaps she'd misjudged him. Misjudged the depth of the chemistry between them. Misjudged his infinite self-control. The old feeling of not being good enough swamped her, but just as she might have withdrawn he hauled her up onto her toes and claimed her mouth with his.

Ava sighed blissfully against his lips. Her body knew his, trusted his. When he groaned and slanted his mouth to widen hers she didn't even think of holding back. She had wanted him to touch her—had wanted to touch him—for weeks, and it felt as if her whole body just melted into his like a boneless mass.

Possibly she was just being driven by the need to be physically close to someone right now. The ghosts of those she had loved and lost lay heavy in her heart after her horrifying ordeal. But she didn't care. She had never wanted a man the way she wanted James Wolfe.

'I want you, Ava.' His voice was as rough as a cat's tongue against her ear. 'God knows I've tried to resist you. Tried and failed. If you don't stop me now I won't be able to.'

Ava gazed into eyes as black as the night sky outside. He was giving her a message, she knew it. He wasn't the one for her no matter how good it felt to be with him.

Maybe it would have been smarter to heed that warning. Maybe it would have been smarter to push him away. But her body refused to cooperate. Something inside her sensed that he needed her equally as much as she needed him, and that feeling was stronger than any maybe.

'I don't want you to stop.'

CHAPTER ELEVEN

It was as if those passion-drugged words had unleashed a beast inside him. Wolfe forgot all about the gut-wrenching pain in his back and instead could only feel the gut-wrenching ache in his body. For her. Only for her.

Before, when she'd looked at him so guilelessly and told him that everyone needed someone, he had vehemently denied that he did. But right now his body made a mockery of those words. Her concern over his injuries had completely undone him. No woman had ever treated him so tenderly before and it was appalling how badly he wanted to soak that up.

As if in a dream state Wolfe smoothed his hands down over her thighs, encouraging them up around his hips. 'Put your legs around my waist.' His voice was so rough it was barely recognisable as he hoisted her higher.

'I hate it when you get macho,' she teased, locking her ankles together and squeezing his hips.

Wolfe's eyelids grew heavy as he felt her heat against his abdomen. Her breathlessness inflamed him even further. 'You want me to put mine around yours?'

Her husky laugh turned into a low, keening cry as he adjusted her so that she rocked against his erection exactly where he knew she needed it the most. A deep sense of satisfaction hit him hard at the thought that he could please this spirited woman so easily.

He kissed her all the way back to his room, only breaking contact to switch on the side lamp and lie her back on his bed.

This was what he wanted—what he had dreamt of since Gilles's wedding. Ava, hot for him. Spread out on his bed, aroused and waiting for him to take her. To possess her.

The warning in his head that he wanted her just a little too much was driven out by the sheer, unequivocal desire to take and brand her as his own.

Forgetting all about technique and—heaven help him—finesse, he pulled the front her shirt open, uncaring as some of the buttons tore free.

Her breath caught, pushing her breasts higher. Her nipples were already standing up and begging for his mouth. 'I need a shower.'

'No.' He shook his head slowly, his eyes drinking in her naked perfection. 'You need me.'

And he needed her. So badly it was a physical pain. He needed to be inside her and he gave up trying to work out why.

When she was naked, spread out before him like this, it would take a whole army to pull him off her, and he had the insane urge to beat his chest and chain her to the bed so that she could never leave.

More than a little disturbed by that gut-wrenching notion, Wolfe shoved it aside along with his jeans. Nothing, not even the whispered warnings of self-preservation in his head, was going to stop him from taking her now. He climbed over the top of her, his mouth nipping her skin wherever it landed.

Her hands stroked up his arms, trying to pull him down over her, but he resisted. He had no intention of rushing this. Instead he straddled her hips, imprisoning her legs with his and brought his hands up to cup and pleasure her breasts.

She tried to arch into his caress, but she was effectively trapped and he smiled. 'I know you hate this type of macho stuff.' He lightly brushed over her nipples as if by accident, enjoying that little catch in her breath. 'So feel free to tell me to stop at any time.'

Her eyes flew open. 'I should…I should…'

She stopped breathing again as he circled ever closer to her rigid peaks. She squirmed, making his erection throb, but he deliberately held off giving her what she wanted—what he wanted—building the anticipation between them, making them both burn.

Her hands stroked down over his chest towards his throbbing erection, a look of power and delight tilting her smile.

'Uh-uh.' He secured both her wandering hands in one of his above her head and dropped a kiss on her open mouth, lingering long enough to tease her with his tongue.

'You said "I",' he reminded her.

'I will never speak to you again if you don't put yourself inside me right now,' she vowed.

'What about this?' he asked, watching her face as he rolled a nipple between his thumb and forefinger.

She sighed in rapture, her body tightening as if she was a weapon he was fine-tuning.

He let go of her wrists and brought both his hands into play to pleasure her gorgeous breasts. The sight of her like that was highly erotic. He let his eyes roam over her flushed face and chest, enjoying her pleasure as he slowly increased the pressure to a torturous level.

'Oh, that. Oh, yes. Don't stop. Wolfe!'

Her arms fluttered and moved down, her hands sculpting his chest and abdomen until finally one was cupping him while the other palmed his aroused length. The bandages on her palms were cool where her fingers were hot. He bit back a pleasurable oath, his eyes closing as he continued to tug on her sweet nipples and absorbed her sensual touch at the same time.

'Wait,' he advised softly. 'Ava, baby, if you keep doing that I'm going to lose control.'

He shifted out of her hold, smiling as the sound of protest she made in the back of her throat turned to relief when he took the tip of her breast into his mouth.

She writhed beneath him and he released her imprisoned legs to stroke his hand between her thighs. She was hot and wet, so close to her climax he could feel the tiny tremors of her release beneath his fingers.

'Not yet, baby. I want to be inside you when you come.'

'I can't help it,' she moaned. 'You've pushed me too far.'

'Not yet, I haven't.' He urged her legs wider and positioned himself at the apex of her body. 'But I intend to.'

On a single powerful thrust he surged deep, pausing just long enough to let her expand around him before moving again. She whimpered desperately and dragged his face down to hers.

A primal sense of satisfaction rushed through him as he established a steady rhythm, rolling his hips against hers and causing a string of sensual spasms throughout her body that sucked him in even deeper.

Driving into her, Wolfe didn't stop until he felt her go still, poised on the edge of her release. He held her there as long as he could, but she moved against him, sobbing as her climax consumed her, her inner contractions forcing his own body to speed towards a release that burned hotter than the West Australian sun.

Wolfe woke and knew instantly that he'd overslept—something he hadn't done since before his army days. And in his arms was a woman who twisted his insides into knots Houdini would struggle to break out of. He thought about his inflexible rules: short, sweet and simple. Only one of them had been upheld last night, and it wasn't short or simple.

He lifted a strand of her hair and closed his eyes as he breathed in the soft floral fragrance, ignoring the screaming pain in his back from muscles still stiff from lack of use.

He'd ignored them the night before, too, when they'd been screaming from overuse. He'd lost track of the amount of times they'd made love, each time eclipsing the last in a way he would have said was impossible. And it wasn't just the sex he'd wanted, he realised uneasily. He liked her. He liked spending time with her. Watching her. Listening to her. Being challenged by her. Somehow, in a short space of time, she had come to mean more to him than any other woman ever had. More than he wanted her to. More than he was willing to think about.

She gave a small moan and snuggled deeper into his shoulder. Irresistible.

'What time is it?'

He glanced down and smiled as her eyes remained scrunched closed. 'I take it you're not a morning person?'

She rolled onto her back and shifted her head onto the pillow. 'Not really. You?'

'Always.' He propped up on his side. 'In fact I'm never up late, even after spending most of the night awake. I think you're making me soft.'

She glanced briefly down his body. 'I hope not.'

Wolfe gave a chuckle. 'Witch,' he said against her mouth, and her lips opened under his in a way that made him think about taking her again.

Remember the rules, a timely voice reminded him forcefully.

Yeah, the rules. The ones he was breaking faster than a politician broke election promises.

He jumped out of bed and reached for the jeans he'd discarded on the floor the night before. 'How about you take a minute to wake up while I fix something to eat?'

'Oh, Wolfe, your back looks terrible.'

He glanced over his shoulder. 'It'll heal.' He yanked a T-shirt over his head and his belly clenched as he saw Ava staring in that region. 'How are your hands?'

'*Quoi?*'

He couldn't prevent a crooked smile from curling one side of his mouth when she looked at him with dazed eyes. 'Your hands? How are they?'

She made a great show of looking at them, but he suspected she was trying to hide her blush from him. She never blushed, as far as he knew, and the sight was pleasing on a purely male level.

'Sore.'

'I'll take a look at them after breakfast,' he promised, grasping her wrists lightly and dropping a kiss against each bandage before he thought better of it.

Ava paused in the doorway of the kitchen and watched Wolfe flip something in the frying pan. His lithe, narrow-hipped frame drew her eye like a flame drew a moth.

He turned as if sensing her and gave her a lazy grin. 'The clothes fit, then?'

Ava glanced down at the oversized T-shirt and board shorts she'd had to roll twice at the waist to keep them up. 'I think that might be a grave exaggeration, but they're not falling off.'

His gaze lingered on her legs. 'Eggs, bacon.' He cleared his throat. 'Tomatoes in two minutes. It's not *nouvelle cuisine.*'

'I don't need anything fancy,' she assured him.

He gave her such an open, clear-eyed smile before turning back to the stove that Ava felt something inside her shift and fall into place. Shell-shocked, she couldn't move.

She loved him.

She had been trying to ignore the feelings burbling away inside her for so long but…*mon Dieu*, she had loved him from that first night. Had she? A lump rose in her throat as she recalled how gentle he had been with her mother's cat. At the time she'd told him that she hated him but she hadn't. Not even then.

'You okay?'

Ava glanced up from the terracotta tiles to find Wolfe holding a spatula and wearing a frown. 'Fine.'

'Well, that's a surefire answer saying that you're not.'

'No. I am.' She strolled into the room as if she hadn't just made a discovery that would irrevocably change her for ever. She couldn't tell him. Not only were her emotions too new, she didn't know how to tell him. And she was pretty sure he wasn't feeling the same thing she was, so she smiled instead. 'Really. I was just thinking of last night.'

'Good to know I make you scowl.'

'The other part.'

'Come here.' He pulled her in close. Kissed her mouth.

His warmth made her heart swell but she didn't let herself think it was more than it was. 'The eggs are burning,' she said faintly, wanting space.

His gaze was piercing, as if he was trying to read her, and she painted on another smile. 'I'll get the orange juice.'

'I've made fresh coffee, as well.'

Coffee. Yes. That would help her jumbled thoughts.

She opened the fridge. Funny, but when she had imagined realising she was in love with someone it hadn't been anything like this. She'd imagined she might be at a restaurant, or in bed, somewhere cosy, wrapped up in her lover's embrace. One of them would say it and then the other…they'd smile, share the moment…

'It's right there.'

Ava started as Wolfe reached around her and pulled a carton from the door, his other hand resting on the small of her back.

'Are you sure you're okay?'

'Positive.' Positive she might never be okay again. That was what she was positive about. Because Wolfe wouldn't want her love. He wasn't a man who wanted any woman's love. In fact if she told him how she felt it would probably send him running in the other direction.

* * *

Ava pulled her foot up onto a wooden chair and hooked her arm around her knee, nursing what remained of her coffee in both hands. They'd decided to eat their food outside by the infinity pool, but although the view was magnificent she had barely paid it any attention.

'So, tell me why you joined the army,' she asked, intrigued by some of the stories he'd told her about the time he'd spent with Gilles when they were younger.

Wolfe set down his fork and pushed his empty plate away, reaching for his own coffee. He took his time stretching out his long legs, his jeans riding so low she could just see the ridge of that fascinating muscle that wrapped around his hipbones where his T-shirt didn't quite cover him.

'Couldn't think of anything else to do with my time.'

'Really?' She dragged her eyes back to his face as if she hadn't just been ogling him. She didn't believe a man with his keen intelligence would make such a decision so casually. If she had to guess she'd say it had something to do with his need to protect everyone around him. Like his brother. His father. 'That was it?'

His eyes narrowed, as if he could discern her thoughts. 'Don't make me out to be some sort of hero, Ava, because I'm not.'

Even without the cool words she could see the sudden tension in him and wondered if it was because this was the first personal question she had asked him since that night he had talked about his family.

Trying not to let his response completely ruin the mood between them, Ava cast her eyes over the golden cliff-faces and tiered flowerbeds that tripped down towards a horseshoe-shaped blue lagoon. 'Wow, this view is really something. Is the whole island this beautiful?'

'The other side gets the wind straight off the Atlantic, so it's a bit scrubbier, but basically yes.'

'Do you come here often?'

'Not as often as I'd like.'

Ava sighed. 'It's so relaxing here. It's as if the real world is another planet. If I had my way I'd stay for ever.'

The scrape of wood against terracotta brought her eyes back to him.

'It's deceptively dangerous. That cove down there is relatively sheltered, but the island can get twenty-five-foot waves at times, and then the beaches are littered with seaweed.'

His tone was much darker than it needed to be and Ava suspected he was talking about more than just the island. She suspected it was a warning for her not to fall for him, but if it was it was not only too late but completely unnecessary. What did he think she was going to do? Stalk him?

'And speaking of for ever...we didn't use protection last night.'

Ah, so *that* was what had triggered his tension. Ava felt her stomach bottom out. She hadn't even thought of it. She'd been so absorbed by her feelings for him, by her anxiety about what to do...

'I can see you're shocked.' He gathered up their plates, the harsh sound of cutlery sliding against porcelain jarring her. 'If you're pregnant it will change things.'

She *was* shocked—but more because the prospect didn't make her nearly as unhappy as he thought. In fact it made her feel elated to think of herself carrying his child. Something she definitely wasn't prepared to admit when his face had taken on all the levity of a thundercloud.

'What do you mean?' And still her silly, hopeful heart beat just a little faster as she waited for him to declare his love for her. Ask her to marry him.

'You'll have to cancel any plans you have to marry the Prince of Triole, for one thing.'

Quoi?

Ava stared at him. He thought she was going to marry Lorenzo? And he'd still slept with her! Controlling her temper by a thread, Ava arched her brow. 'No?'

One of the knives on the plate he was holding clattered onto the tiles but neither one of them broke eye contact to locate it. 'No. You'll be marrying me.'

'*You?*' She hadn't expected him to say that and it threw her off balance. 'I already told you I wouldn't marry without love.'

He paused, his brows pulled together. 'Not even for a child?'

Dull colour flooded her cheeks and a breeze rustled the nearby shrubs. Trap a man who so clearly wanted his freedom? 'I'd rather be a single parent.'

He glared at her. 'Since I don't hold the same view you'd better hope you're not pregnant. Because if you are you *will* marry me, Ava.'

'You'd better hope you're not pregnant. Because if you are you will *marry me.'*

Wolfe leaned his elbows on his desk and cupped his face in his hands. What an idiot.

Before, when she'd been sitting on his deck, he'd been looking at her and thinking how lovely she was. How much he enjoyed having her in his home. In his life. Then she'd mentioned for ever and he'd broken out in a cold sweat. It was as if she'd read his mind.

Panicked, he realised that in making breakfast and playing house with her he was not only still breaking all his rules with her but grinding them into the dust for good measure. This must have been how his father had felt about his mother. How else to explain why he'd taken her back over and over? Wolfe had vowed never to let a woman mean so much to him that she weakened him in the same way. But that had nothing to do with Ava, did it?

Hell, he'd acted like an ass and he owed her an apology. A big apology.

After checking once more for updates on the bomb blast that had ripped her gallery in half, he scoured the house and found her walking on the beach.

She was a vision of loveliness, with his large blue T-shirt swamping her lanky frame and her mane of dark hair rippling down her back. Watching her, Wolfe felt a now familiar tug in his chest and knew he was in trouble. Deep trouble.

Not that it would do him any good to think that way. She'd made it pretty clear before that she saw him as nothing more than a temporary entity in her life.

'I'd rather be a single parent.'

Just the thought of her vehemence made him see red. Made his anger— He stopped. Blinked. What the hell was wrong with him? Had a brick from her building landed on his head last night and messed with his brain? Surely nothing else could explain his seesawing emotions.

Ava's soft laugh reached him from across the sand and forced his attention back to the present moment.

She turned slightly to twist her hair out of her face and Wolfe forgot all about his apology when he saw that she was on her phone.

When had she got that? And, more importantly, hadn't he told her not to use it while she was here?

Totally off balance, he let his frustration and volatile emotions morph into savage anger. 'Dammit, are you stupid? You don't make calls on a mobile phone.'

Ava spun round at the sound of Wolfe's harsh voice and nearly dropped her phone in the water. She could still hear Baden's voice but could no longer make out the words, her attention totally focused on the furious expression on Wolfe's face. Her breath caught and she felt as if she was thirteen years old and being confronted by her disapproving father.

'I have to go.' She disconnected the phone just as Wolfe reached her.

'What do you think you're doing?' he said, breathing fire and brimstone at her.

'Ice-skating?'

'Dammit, Ava. I told you not to make mobile phone calls from the island.'

She frowned, pretty sure that he hadn't. 'No, you didn't.'

'Yes. I. Did.'

'No. You. Did. Not. But anyway I didn't make a call. I received one.' She'd found her phone on Wolfe's chest of drawers after breakfast and checking her messages had helped take her mind off just how futile her feelings for him were.

'Answering it works the same way,' he said through gritted teeth. 'It gives away our location to anyone with the equipment to utilise it.'

'You use yours,' she felt stung into retorting.

'Mine's encrypted.'

Ava shoved her hands on her hips. 'Well, nobody told me that.'

Wolfe shook his head and ground his jaw as if she were a complete imbecile. 'I *knew* this wouldn't work.'

'I have no idea what you're referring to, but I've had enough of your overbearing attitude for one day,' she fumed. 'And, so you don't have to worry, it was just Baden checking up on me after the bomb. I hope that is not against your rules?'

She stalked off in the direction of the house. This was exactly like her father, judging her and finding her lacking. It hurt. Despite everything she had promised herself she had given Wolfe the power to hurt her. She had no one else to blame but herself.

As she passed the pool she glanced down at the phone in her hand and in a fit of pique her father would say was incredibly impulsive tossed it into the water.

'Dammit, that was a fool thing to do.'

She spun around, not realising that Wolfe had followed so

closely behind her. 'Like climbing that dumb wall at Gilles's. I wish I'd never done that either. Maybe then we would never have met.'

'We would have met.'

Caught off guard by his brooding tone, she felt all her anger leave her body and for a minute stood in front of him feeling strangely lost.

She needed a cup of tea. Yes, that would help her regroup. She glanced once more at the rippling pool as she stalked off. It *had* been stupid to toss her phone in it, particularly since she still had messages to check.

'What are you doing now?'

Ava opened a cupboard near the kitchen sink in search of mugs. 'Making tea. Do you want some?'

'No. The cups are above your head.'

'Do you have lemon verbena, by any chance?'

Wolfe expelled a long breath and some of the tension seemed to leach out of him. 'I have no idea.' He strode to a cupboard and started rifling through containers. 'No. Will peppermint do?'

'Yes.' Their eyes connected. Held. 'Thank you.'

Wolfe watched her pour boiling water into a mug and berated himself for letting his frustration at the situation cloud his objectivity. No wonder he hadn't located her brother's killer yet.

And she'd been right before. He *hadn't* told her not to use her phone. He'd *meant* to. But that wasn't the same thing. And mistakes like that got people killed.

Could get her killed.

Now he'd have to change their location. Find another safe place. Because he wouldn't risk her life, no matter how small the chance that the killer had the skills to track her to the island. He didn't know who he was dealing with and it was time to act as if he had some sort of a clue as to how to do his job.

He blew out a breath.

He needed to apologise to her. Again.

Without giving himself time to decide if it was a bad idea, he wrapped his arms around her from behind.

She stiffened but he didn't let go.

'I'm sorry for yelling at you. I behaved like a jackass.'

'Yes, you did.' She sniffed. 'Why?'

Now, there was the million-dollar question. 'I was jealous.'

Her eyebrows shot up. 'Of Baden?'

'I thought you were talking to Lorenzo.'

Her eyes softened and Wolfe felt more vulnerable than he ever had, even as a kid walking up to the front door of his house after school and wondering if his mother would be home.

Her throat worked and he was sure she was about to say something soft and mushy. He wanted to hear it so badly he ducked his head and kissed her breathless. He wasn't sure if she had been about to tell him that she loved him but he couldn't have coped if she had.

Because it wouldn't be real. They had grown closer through forced proximity and sex, but that wasn't love. And he couldn't bear to hear her say it when she didn't mean it.

A memory of his mother tucking him into bed and kissing his forehead when he was about five punched him in the head. Her warmth…her soft touch…

He felt a yearning open up inside him and doused it by slipping his hands beneath Ava's baggy T-shirt and appeasing a much more basic need. He stroked her breasts until she arched into him.

This.

This was something he knew he could trust in.

He lifted her onto the bench and yanked the shorts down her long legs, shifting her forward so that his erection was cradled in the notch between her thighs.

'That feels so good,' she groaned, wrapping her arms around his neck.

Wolfe kissed her like a starving man and carried her back to his bedroom.

'After the bomb?'

'Mmm?' Ava felt Wolfe shift to his side and let her body collapse against him.

'Ava, baby, wake up. I need to ask you something.'

'Mmm? Do I have to?'

'Yes, come on, baby. Back to the land of the living.' She sighed, enjoying the way his hand stroked her hair from her face.

'Okay, I'm back, General. What it is you want to know?'

'You said before that Baden was checking on you after the bomb?'

Ava frowned. The urgency in his voice was more than clear. 'Yes.'

'Did you tell him about it?'

'No.'

'You're sure? Now, think, baby. I need you to be certain.'

'I'm not a child, Wolfe.'

'Don't go getting surly on me again.'

She arched a brow. 'Me? Get surly?'

'Okay, okay.' He cupped her face in his hands. 'This is important. I need you to be one hundred percent certain.'

'Why would I tell Baden when he already knew about it?'

Wolfe closed his eyes briefly, as if he was in pain. Which he might be considering his bruises and their recent lovemaking. 'He shouldn't know.'

Ava pushed his hands aside, the nape of her neck tingling. 'I don't see how he couldn't. It must be all over the media, and my father would have told him.'

Before she'd even finished speaking Wolfe was off the

bed, shucking into his boxers and jeans. 'Dammit, where's my phone?'

'I saw it in the kitchen. Wolfe…?'

'Stay here.'

Ava stared after his departing figure and only paused to sweep up the T-shirt he hadn't bothered to put on before racing after him.

He was on the phone but speaking too quietly for her to take in more than, "Yeah…" and, "Get back to me."

'Want to tell me what's going on?'

Wolfe had his soldier's face on when he turned to her. 'You might want to sit down.'

Ava did, but only because his intensity was starting to make her legs feel rubbery. 'You think it's Baden.'

Wolfe pulled a chair in front of hers and sat down, his hands gentle as he held hers. 'I know you don't want to believe this, but your father just confirmed that Baden hadn't been told about the explosion.'

'But it must be all over the internet by now at the very least.'

He shook his head. 'No. I had it suppressed. As far as anyone knows a car ran into the front of your gallery.'

Ava stared at Wolfe's hands, absently noting how beautiful they were. Then her eyes rose to his. 'Baden would never have hurt Frédéric.'

Wolfe sighed. 'I'm sorry, Ava. I know you won't want to hear this but my team have been closing in on him for a few days now. He's mentally unstable. Did you know that?'

Mentally unstable? Ava shook her head.

'He's been diagnosed with schizophrenia. And his psychological transcripts reveal that he blames your father for the death of his.'

Stunned by what he was telling her, Ava shook her head. 'No. His father died in a boating accident.'

'Your father was driving it.'

'I know, but… You think Baden believes *he* should be the heir to the throne in Anders?'

'That's what it looks like.'

'But why do something now? Why not get rid of me and Frédéric years ago?'

'He might not have considered it. He might be off his meds. Or perhaps your father's illness has made him panic.'

Ava refused to countenance Wolfe's ideas.

'How could he expect to get away with such a thing?'

'That's the part only he knows.'

His expression grew remote and she felt him mentally withdraw from her when he stood up.

'All you need to know is that it's over. You can go home.'

CHAPTER TWELVE

'IT'S OVER. *You can go home.*'

Ava shivered. She knew Wolfe meant more than the threat to her life was over, and it made the four-hour flight to Anders interminable. She spent the whole time thinking about every way imaginable to tell him that she loved him and didn't want him to leave, but came up empty.

She'd nearly blurted it out in his kitchen, when he'd told her he was jealous, but he'd tensed up like a lone lion with a pack of hungry hyenas approaching and distracted her. She suspected that move had been because he had guessed what she'd been about to say and didn't want to hear it. And why would he? It wasn't as if she would be giving him some prized gift he'd waited his whole life to receive.

And on top of that her period had arrived midflight. She didn't know how she felt about that, having thought all afternoon about what it would be like to carry Wolfe's baby. But she knew she hadn't been relieved to find his bathroom well stocked with female hygiene products. Though that had been a timely reminder that he was a man who enjoyed women. And plenty of them. And knowing why, knowing that his mother had left him over and over and no doubt given him a healthy dose of abandonment issues in the process, didn't make the reality of his choices any easier to bear.

Still feeling torn about what to do when the plane finally

landed, she moved to the open doorway and paused. A fierce wind whipped her hair around her head. She saw her father and, surprisingly, Lorenzo waiting beside one of the palace cars, and she wished she was wearing more than one of Wolfe's shirts tied in a knot at the waist and a pair of his jeans rolled at both ends.

She felt Wolfe come up behind her and turned, expecting that he would accompany her down onto the tarmac. As soon as she saw the remote expression on his face she knew instantly that he wasn't going to. And, unlike the last time he had flown her home, she would have welcomed his support now.

'You're not coming,' she said unnecessarily, straightening her spine as if his actions meant nothing to her.

Wolfe hesitated and then shook his head. 'No. I have another job to go to.'

Oh. She hadn't thought of that. 'Where is it?'

'That's confidential.'

And dangerous. He didn't have to add that.

Ava gripped the inside of the open doorway, remembering all those scars on his body.

'I won't be back.'

She nodded slowly, feeling as if her stomach was about to upend its entire contents all over his shiny shoes. He looked at her warily, as if he was expecting her to kick up a fuss and stamp her feet—beg him to stay, perhaps. And she wanted to. She wanted to do all those things. But she wouldn't.

For one thing her father was waiting with what looked like the entire police force in attendance, and for another...Wolfe was too closed. Too distant.

Saying *I love you* seemed like too big a leap to make in the face of his implacable regard, and it wasn't as if it would change the outcome in any way. He was leaving. He couldn't make that any plainer.

'I can see that.'

His eyes snapped to hers, as if he was surprised by her lack of argument. 'I can't give you what you want, Ava. I'm sorry.'

He was sorry?

Ava shook her head at his pitiful comment. No way was she accepting that cop-out. 'How do you know? You haven't even asked what I want.' She knew there was an edge of frustration in her voice but she couldn't contain it. 'The truth is, Wolfe, you don't want to give me what I want because you have trained yourself not to need anyone. To be like that island you own. But you're not, and if you're honest with yourself you'll realise that your mother's actions hurt you just as much as they did your brother. Maybe more.'

She glanced up quickly, wondering if her words had affected him at all. If he got just how ruthlessly he'd disconnected himself emotionally.

'I'm fine as I am.'

That would be a no, then…

Ava sighed. He really was like an immovable rock, and she realised there was nothing left to say. The fact was Wolfe didn't love her and, as she had so often had to do lately, she had to face the reality of her situation.

Closing her eyes briefly against the quivering sensation in her bottom lip, she straightened her spine, marshalling her indifference to protect herself as she had so often done in the past. But it wasn't easy. Wolfe had crashed through her protective walls with the force of a military tank and all she wanted was for him to take her in his arms and tell her he loved her.

'Okay, then.' She turned to go, her feet leaden.

She hadn't made it two steps when he grabbed hold of her arm and stopped her. Ava felt her heart soar and searched his face for some sign that he was about to—

'You'll let me know if there's a child, won't you?' His voice was gravelly, strained.

Right then her hopes and dreams were well and truly shattered. She knew he would have 'done the right thing' if she *had* been pregnant, and it was with some irony that she realised that while she had fought marrying someone else for convenience she had never considered that the opposite could happen. That someone would have to marry *her* for convenience.

'There won't be,' she replied woodenly.

He frowned and dropped her arm. 'You can't know that for sure.'

'Yes, I can,' she said wearily. 'I got my period on the plane. Nice stash of female hygiene products, by the way.'

'My staff stock my plane, not me.'

Okay, that was something…sort of.

When he didn't immediately walk away she glanced up again and found his expression fierce.

'Ava, I still want you.'

She stared back at him while those words sank in and then she just felt angry. 'I don't know what you want me to say to that, Wolfe.' Because apart from begging him to stay what could she say? That he should do what she wanted him to do? Be what she wanted him to be? Wasn't that what she had railed against her father for her whole life? 'It doesn't mean anything. It's only lust and lust fades over time. Isn't that what you believe?'

'Yes.'

God, she hoped he was right. Because she felt as if her heart was being cleaved in half with a toothpick.

'Ava?' Her father materialised at her side. 'Is there a problem?'

'No.' Swallowing hard, she braced herself to look at Wolfe one more time, her eyes tracking over his features like a laser beam, trying to trace every fine detail of his handsome face. 'Goodbye, Monsieur Wolfe. I hope you find what it is you are searching for.'

Turning away before he saw how painful it was for her

to walk away from him, Ava let her father escort her from the plane, resolved to face whatever the future had in store for her with the same dignity and grace her mother would have shown.

CHAPTER THIRTEEN

WOLFE HAULED HIMSELF out of the sparkling blue sea and flopped onto the hot sand. The sun beat down on his head with relentless precision and a hermit crab scurried towards the ocean in search of safety.

The only sounds he could hear were the languid ebb and flow of the incoming tide and the intermittent squawk of overhead birds as they dived for fresh fish.

By rights he should have felt happy and relaxed, but he didn't. He hadn't felt that way for three days. Not since flying out of Anders and ordering his pilot to return to Cape Paraiso instead of flying him to the round of meetings he'd had to put off to guard Ava.

Ava.

When he'd left her back in Anders he had somehow convinced himself that he would be fine. That he would get over her. Right now he felt very far from fine. And his sense of loss when she'd told him she had got her monthly period on the plane made a mockery of his assertion that he would get over her.

'I hope you find what it is you're searching for,' she had said at the end.

The trouble was he hadn't been searching for anything. She'd been right in her first assumption that night at the gala ball. He was running. Filling up his life with work and activities so he would never have to face how empty his existence really was. So he'd never have to think about what he really wanted.

But that was unavoidable now, it seemed, because he couldn't think about anything else. He couldn't think about anything other than Ava.

He shook water from his hair and let his hands dangle over his knees.

The fact was he missed her.

She was everywhere on the island. In his kitchen in the morning when he made coffee, on his deck when he stood beside the pool and searched for the silver phone he'd removed a week ago, in his bed at night when he rolled over and found it empty, on the beach... He wasn't sure how she had infiltrated every part of his mind so profoundly in such a short space of time but there was no doubting that she had.

And if he kept up obsessing about her like this the next thing he'd think was that he was in love with her.

Hell.

He *was* in love with her.

Why keep denying it? He'd known it for a long time—he'd just refused to face it. Fear had kept him immobile. Fear of needing her more than she needed him. Fear of ending up a lonely shell of a man like his father. Fear of facing the fact that, yes, he *had* been just as devastated as his brother every time his mother had done her disappearing act.

'Understood what, Wolfe? That you were a child who couldn't rely on his mother's love?'

Oh, hell.

His heart had known the truth. His heart had kept pushing him towards her. His heart had wanted to protect her and care for her. His heart had insisted that he trash his dodgy rules every time he'd looked at her. It was his head that had come late to the party.

But was it too late?

Wolfe stared blankly out to sea. The way he saw it he had two options. He could take the risk, tell her how he felt and hope she didn't have guards cart him away, or he could keep his pride intact, travelling the world by himself until he slowly did become that empty shell of a man he had spent his life trying not to be.

He ran his hand through his hair. Hell, that wasn't even a real choice.

'I think we should make the announcement about your engagement to Lorenzo at the same time.'

Ava paused in the middle of scanning the acceptance speech she would read after her father announced his impending abdication and stared at him. 'I disagree.'

'It makes sense to combine the two. It's more efficient.'

Ava's lips pinched together. 'That may be so, but I need to do this my way.'

Her father made a grievous noise that sounded suspiciously like a snort of disgust, but he didn't push it, fussing instead with his military uniform before heading off to the state room where invited guests and the media waited for their arrival.

After double-checking her own outfit—a royal sash pinned diagonally to a satin gown—Ava followed him.

In the past few days they had grown closer than they'd ever been, drawn together by the devastating impact of Baden's actions and a mutual commitment to ensure that he received the best psychiatric care possible. Her father had shown great fortitude in the face of his nephew's betrayal, and Ava wished that she could grant her father this last request of her. But how could she?

Not only did it go against all of her hopes and dreams for herself, but her heart was so heavy she couldn't imagine she'd ever be happy again.

Wasn't it only fair that she worked to get over Wolfe before making the ultimate commitment to another man? Even if that man knew she didn't love him?

But, really, she asked herself, did it matter? Her father's illness had worsened with the stress of everything that had happened, and he was being forced to abdicate. Anders needed an heir... She sighed and came to a stop behind her father's straight figure as he waited for the state room door to be opened. Her pining for unrequited love seemed trivial by comparison.

And Lorenzo was a wonderful man. He would make any woman an excellent husband, and maybe if she committed herself to him the pain of losing Wolfe would start to fade.

'Okay.' She stayed her father with her hand on his arm just before he entered the room. 'Announce it.'

Her father frowned and swiped at the beads of sweat on his brow. Then he nodded. 'You've made me very proud.'

Ava gave a small smile. She hoped her mother had heard that.

Thirty minutes later the large room was buzzing with energy after her father officially announced that Ava would be taking over as Queen in exactly a month's time. Ava's own speech, pledging to uphold and expand on her father's absolute dedication to their country, had been a resounding success. The funny thing was she hadn't once felt nervous or overwhelmed. Either she was more ready to take on this job than she had thought, or all of her nerves had been cauterised when she had walked away from Wolfe.

'And on top of that—' The King waited for the crowd to subside into silence. 'On top of that it is with great pleasure that I also announce—'

'Before you do, Your Majesty, I need a word with your daughter.'

Ava glanced up and gasped as Wolfe strode into the room, the outer door swinging closed behind him. Every head swivelled towards his voice and two of her father's personal guards rushed him—only to fall back when they recognised who he was.

Ava's traitorous heart recognised who he was as well, and started beating heavily in her chest. Her eyes ate him up exactly like that first morning when she had met him as she sat on top of that wall at Château Verne. Only this time he wasn't on a white horse and he wasn't wearing jodhpurs. Instead he stood before her in a business suit and tie that did little to civilise the lethal glint in his golden-brown eyes.

Her father scowled at the interruption and Lorenzo shifted nervously at her other side.

'This had better be good, Wolfe,' her father said.

'It is.' Wolfe's eyes never left hers. 'Ava?'

Ava's heart did a mini-somersault at his commanding tone; shock and surprise that he was standing directly in front of her was making her feel light-headed.

'Surely whatever you have to say to my daughter can wait until after these proceedings are over?' her father said impatiently.

'Not if you're about to announce what I think you are,' Wolfe returned emphatically.

His expression was perfectly urbane but it reminded Ava of the time he had threatened to drag her behind his horse weeks ago. She knew it would be pointless to argue with him in this mood—at least in public. 'It's okay, Father. I'll speak with Monsieur Wolfe in private.'

Lorenzo half rose out of his seat, as if he might object, but one look from Wolfe had him reluctantly subsiding.

'Just tell me this.' Wolfe rounded on her as soon as the footman had closed the door to the small salon she had chosen further down the hall. 'Are you marrying Lorenzo because you love him or because your father wants you to?'

Ava frowned at him. 'Since I know your earlier experiences have given you a very skewed view of how women can be, I'm going to let that slide. But you need to know that question is incredibly insulting to me.'

Wolfe surprised her by shaking his head and laughing. 'Princess, you do have a special way of bringing me back down to size. But the fact that you didn't answer with an emphatic *I love him* gives me hope.'

'Hope about what?'

'Hope that there's still a chance I can convince you to fall in love with me.'

Ava stared at him blankly and then blinked as his words stopped spinning inside her head. 'Why would you want me to do that? You don't even believe in love,' she challenged softly.

A rueful smile formed on his lips. 'I didn't until I met you.'

'You're not making any sense.' Ava didn't dare let her mind head down the track it had veered on to in case the excited beating of her heart was wrong. 'What does that mean?'

It took him three long strides to reach her, and when he did he gripped her fingers in his, his eyes searching hers. 'It means you have opened my eyes to everything that has been missing in my life and why. It means I've been a fool to even think that I could let you walk out of my life.'

He stopped and she watched his throat work as he swallowed, a fleeting moment of nervousness crossing his face.

'It means that I love you, Ava. More than I ever thought possible.'

Ava's mind felt as if it was churning through butter as he said words she'd stopped letting herself imagine would ever fall from his lips. 'Are you serious?'

'About loving you?'

She nodded, lost for words.

Wolfe's lips twisted into a wry smile. 'Absolutely. But I don't blame you for doubting me. I fought my feelings for you the whole way—imagining that they would weaken me, imagining that you would be as flighty and as unpredictable as my mother.'

'I'm not like her, Wolfe,' Ava assured him vehemently. 'I would never abandon my husband. *My child.*'

'I know you wouldn't, baby. You need to know that when I was younger—about twelve or thirteen—and out looking for my brother for the hundredth time, I made a promise to myself that I would never let myself fall in love. That I would never make myself that vulnerable. And until that bright blue-sky morning at Gilles's wedding I've never had cause to reconsider that promise.' He paused, drew her hands up to his lips. 'Then I saw you and…you simply stole the breath from my lungs.'

'You left before I woke up that first morning,' she reminded him.

'That would be one of those foolish moments I was referring to,' he said a little sheepishly. 'And I'm sorry I hurt you. Truthfully, the way you made me feel scared me senseless. Just looking at you makes me burn up with need. When I woke with your head on my shoulder…I admit it—I panicked.'

Ava gave him a lopsided smile. 'I did think it was nice when you fixed my phone.'

'And that was when the trouble really started. After you got the news about your brother you became so withdrawn and I didn't know how to reach you. I tried to tell myself that I didn't want to, but I couldn't stay away from you, Ava. I thought about you constantly.'

'Why didn't you call?' she demanded fiercely.

'Because I didn't *want* to think about you constantly.' He groaned. 'I was still fighting the inevitable at that time…but that's done. Gone.'

'And you don't like talking about the past.'

He loosened his grip on her hands and hauled her into his arms. 'I don't like dwelling on it. But you've shown me that ignoring it doesn't work either. What I want is to learn from it and move forward. I love you, Ava—heart and soul. I want to be with you always. I want to protect you. I want to be the man you turn to when you're busy and… Aw, hell.' He swiped an unsteady hand through his hair. 'When you walked off my plane the other day you took my dead heart with you and made me realise that not only couldn't I live without it, but I didn't want to.'

Ava felt her love for him swell up to the point of overpowering her. 'Oh, Wolfe, I think I've loved you for ever.'

'Thank God.' Wolfe released a pent-up breath and bent to kiss her. 'I think you just made me the happiest man on earth, and there's only one way you could possibly eclipse that.' He reached inside his breast pocket and withdrew a square box. 'It probably doesn't compare to the Crown Jewels in your vault, but I hope you will accept it, baby, as a declaration of just how much you mean to me.'

Ava gasped as she shakily opened the box and saw a ring—a huge navy blue sapphire with two sparkling diamonds on either side.

Wolfe removed it and steadied her hand before slipping it onto her finger. 'Perfect. I knew the colour would match your eyes.'

'Oh, Wolfe.' Ava hugged him tightly, huge shiny tears blurring her vision. 'It's beautiful, and of course I'll accept it, but…' She stopped, suddenly realising the enormity of what he was setting himself up for.

'But what?' His eyes scanned her face. 'If you have a problem I'll fix it.'

'It's not me, Wolfe, it's you.' She gazed at the huge rock on her finger before forcing herself to meet his eyes. 'You probably don't know this yet, but my father has just announced that he'll be abdicating in a month and—oh, *non*!' She squirmed in his arms until he released her enough for her feet to touch the ground once again. 'My father is waiting for me!'

Wolfe buried his face in her hair. 'Wriggling around in my arms like that isn't exactly the quickest way to get back to him. I've missed you,' he admitted huskily.

'And I've missed you. But I have to go to him. You know what he's like. If I don't he'll most likely announce my engagement to Lorenzo without me!'

'He won't.'

'How do you know that? Everyone must be talking. Wondering what is going on.'

'Any fool back there who saw my face knows exactly what's going on. And your father is no fool.'

Talking about her father reminded Ava of her earlier concern and she stilled. 'Wolfe, if you take me on you have to know that your life will change dramatically. You'll have to become a citizen of Anders. You'll have to—'

'Be your back-up person. I get it, Ava. I know what marrying you entails and, frankly, I'd want to marry you if we had to build mud brick houses in the middle of the desert for a living.'

Still she hesitated. 'But what about your business? Your travel? I know if you curb your passions you'll end up unhappy, and I couldn't bear for that to happen.'

'Ava.' He cupped her face in his hands. 'You're not listening—which isn't all that surprising—but…' He laughed as she took a playful swipe at him. 'But you should know by now that I don't do anything without working everything out in advance.'

'So what have you worked out, Monsieur General?'

He gave her the lazy smile of a man who had everything he wanted in life. 'My brother loves running Wolfe Inc far more than I ever did, and I only ever travelled to stop myself from having to think about my life. I don't want to do that any more. And you'll need someone by your side. Just as your father wants.'

Ava finally allowed the smile she'd been holding back to beam up at him, so happy she felt as if her heart was aching with joy. She tightened her arms around his neck. 'You know, in my wildest dreams I imagined love could be just like this.'

Wolfe shook his head. 'My wildest dreams never even gave me a glimpse of this level of happiness. You did that, Ava. You filled a gap in my heart I never even knew existed, and I want you to know that I will be yours for ever.'

Ava gave him a watery smile. She caught the serious undertone to his words and knew that she could trust this man not only with her life but with her heart. Knew that now he had opened himself fully to her he would never let her down. That he would never leave her.

'Good. Because I love you to pieces, James Wolfe, and I will never leave you.'

Wolfe's hungry gaze burned into hers, but just when she thought for sure he was going to lose some of that inimitable control of his he removed his arms from around her waist and clasped her hand with his.

'We need to hurry up and break the news to your father,' he said roughly. 'I've never been a patient man and, as lovely as you look in that dress, it's time you were wearing something else.'

Ava smiled slowly, basking in the glow of Wolfe's unguarded love. 'And do you have something specific in mind?'

'Oh, yeah.' He tugged on her hand and brought her up against him for one brief, soul-deep kiss. 'Me.'

* * * * *

Look out for
Mills & Boon® TEMPTED™ 2-in-1s,
from September

*Fresh, contemporary romances
to tempt all lovers of
great stories*

A sneaky peek at next month...

MODERN™

INTERNATIONAL AFFAIRS, SEDUCTION & PASSION GUARANTEED

My wish list for next month's titles...

In stores from 16th August 2013:

☐ Challenging Dante – Lynne Graham

☐ Lost to the Desert Warrior – Sarah Morgan

☐ Never Say No to a Caffarelli – Melanie Milburne

☐ His Ring Is Not Enough – Maisey Yates

☐ A Reputation to Uphold – Victoria Parker

In stores from 6th September 2013:

☐ Captivated by Her Innocence – Kim Lawrence

☐ His Unexpected Legacy – Chantelle Shaw

☐ A Silken Seduction – Yvonne Lindsay

☐ If You Can't Stand the Heat... – Joss Wood

☐ The Rules of Engagement – Ally Blake

Available at WHSmith, Tesco, Asda, Eason, Amazon and Apple

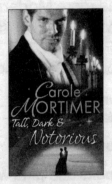

MILLS & BOON®
Book Club

Join the Mills & Boon Book Club

Want to read more **Modern**™ books?
We're offering you **2 more** absolutely **FREE!**

We'll also treat you to these fabulous extras:

- 🌹 **Exclusive offers and much more!**

- 🌹 **FREE home delivery**

- 🌹 **FREE books and gifts with our special rewards scheme**

Get your free books now!

visit www.millsandboon.co.uk/bookclub
or call Customer Relations on 020 8288 2888

The World of Mills & Boon®

There's a Mills & Boon® series that's perfect for you. We publish ten series and, with new titles every month, you never have to wait long for your favourite to come along.

Blaze®
Scorching hot, sexy reads
4 new stories every month

By Request
Relive the romance with the best of the best
9 new stories every month

Cherish™
Romance to melt the heart every time
12 new stories every month

Desire™
Passionate and dramatic love stories
8 new stories every month

Visit us Online